Dear Reader,

It is with much pleasure that I welcome you to my four-book miniseries, MEN OF THE OUTBACK. The setting moves from my usual stamping ground, my own state of Queensland, to the Northern Territory, which is arguably the most colorful and exciting part of the continent. It comprises what we call the Top End and the Red Center—two extreme climatic and geographical divisions. This is what makes the Territory so fascinating. The tropical, World Heritage–listed Kakadu National Park, with crocodiles and water buffalo to the Top, and in the Center the desert—the "dead heart" that's not actually dead at all—only lying dormant until the rains transform it into the greatest garden on earth.

The pervading theme of the series is family. Family offers endless opportunities for its members to hurt and be hurt, to love and support, or bitterly condemn. What sort of family we grew up in reverberates for the rest of our lives. One thing is certain: at the end of the day, *blood* binds.

I invite you, dear reader, to explore the lives of my families. My warmest best wishes to you all.

Margaret Way

MEN OF THE OUTBACK launched with
The Cattleman, Superromance #1328

Look for
Her Outback Protector, Harlequin Romance, #3895
Coming June 2006

"The moment I saw you..." Ross stopped dead before she prized it out of him.

"Yes?" Samantha caught her breath as if on the brink of a revelation.

There was a recklessness in his blood he knew was getting the better of him. She had insinuated herself into his dreams.

He looked at her through the mask he affected. "I knew then I'd have need of protective armor." He turned away, knowing he was leaving her baffled.

"I'd love to know what you were really going to say."

"The fact I even said that makes me wonder."

"It would be really something to see. *You* losing control. You are such an enigma, Ross Sunderland."

"And you're desperate to solve the mystery."

The seductive note in his voice roused her so much he might have suddenly begun to trail a hand over her body.

THE CATTLE
BARON'S BRIDE

Margaret Way

Men of the
Outback

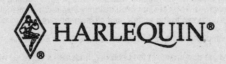

TORONTO • NEW YORK • LONDON
AMSTERDAM • PARIS • SYDNEY • HAMBURG
STOCKHOLM • ATHENS • TOKYO • MILAN • MADRID
PRAGUE • WARSAW • BUDAPEST • AUCKLAND

ISBN 0-373-03891-7

THE CATTLE BARON'S BRIDE

First North American Publication 2006.

This edition published by arrangement with Harlequin Books S.A.

® and TM are trademarks of the publisher. Trademarks indicated with
® are registered in the United States Patent and Trademark Office, the
Canadian Trade Marks Office and in other countries.

www.eHarlequin.com

Printed in U.S.A.

Margaret Way takes great pleasure in her work and works hard at her pleasure. She enjoys tearing off to the beach with her family on weekends, loves haunting galleries and auctions, and is completely given over to French champagne "for every possible joyous occasion." She was born and educated in the river city of Brisbane, Australia, and now lives within sight and sound of beautiful Moreton Bay.

Books by Margaret Way:

HARLEQUIN ROMANCE®
3859—THE OUTBACK ENGAGEMENT†
3863—MARRIAGE AT MURRAREE†

HARLEQUIN SUPERROMANCE®
1328—THE CATTLEMAN††

*Koomera Crossing
†The McIvor Sisters
††Men of the Outback

CHAPTER ONE

BY THE light of the stars alone in a situation fraught with difficulties and dangers Sunderland and his tracker Joe Goolatta led a traumatised jackeroo missing since late afternoon the previous day back through dense tropical jungle to the safety of the savannah. The forest floor was alive with activity. All sorts of nocturnal creatures, some with malevolent eyes, pounced on prey or scuttled under foot hunting for food. Forest debris crashed to the ground as the countless legions of possums with their thick pelts ripped up leaves and twigs or made their prodigious leaps from tree to tree sending down a hailstorm of edible berries and nuts. Huge bats hung upside down assuming the appearance of vampires. Other dark forms flapped over head. Monstrous amethyst pythons growing to twenty feet long wrapped themselves around branches close over head, while the brown snakes and their brothers the deadly black snakes moved slowly, sinuously through the trees guided not by sight but smell as they stalked sleeping birds. Now and again a night bird shrieked an alarm at their presence as they trekked through the forest galleries. Giant epiphytes clung to the buttresses of the rain forest trees, staghorns and elkhorns; all kinds of climbing orchids glimmered in the starlight. Now and again Sunderland slashed at something. Probably the Stinging Tree. Brushing up against the leaves could inflict extreme pain. Sunderland and the tracker scarcely made a sound. They might have spent their whole lives living in this overwhelming stronghold of Nature among the community of rain forest animals. Ben Rankin, the jackeroo, seventeen years old moaned and groaned, his every movement jerky and slow as he stumbled over thick woody prop roots and fallen branches, vines that grew in wild tangles, letting out high pitched nervous cries to rival the shrieks of the night bird.

"Get a hold there, Rankin," Sunderland clipped off, not impressed by the lad's behaviour. He grasped the boy's arm for perhaps the hundredth time giving him a helping hand. "We're nearly there."

How could he possibly know? Ben marvelled. The Boss's night vision was awesome.

Finally they emerged into a clearing having walked unerringly to the very spot where a station jeep was parked. *Who would believe it?*

"Made it!" The old aboriginal stockman spoke with satisfaction. "Must be four, thereabouts," he growled, looking up at the lightening sky. "Not far off sunrise."

"Almost time to start work again," Sunderland said wryly, pushing the hapless jackeroo into the back seat of the jeep where the youngster collapsed into a heap. Ben's whole body was shuddering. He was physically and mentally spent now his ordeal was over. "Oh God, oh God!" he sobbed, covering his head with his hands. "I'm such a fool."

"Too right, little buddy!" the old aboriginal said, making his disgust clear.

Sunderland showed no emotion at all as though it were a sheer waste of time. He put light pressure on the boy's shoulder. "You've had a bad experience. Learn from it."

"Yes, sir." Ben's breath came out like a hiss his jaw was clamped so tight. "Kept thinking a bloody great croc would get me."

Goolatta snorted.

"We're nowhere near the river. Or a billabong for that matter," Sunderland pointed out matter-of-factly, not having a lot of time for the boy's distress either. Rankin like all the other recruits had been obliged to sit in on lectures regarding station safety. He had been warned many times never to hare off on his own. Most had the sense to listen. Territory cattle stations were vast. Some as big as European countries. It was dead easy to get lost in the relatively featureless wilderness. Obeying the rules made the difference between living and dying. A few over the years had disappeared without trace.

"When you realised you were lost you should have stayed put instead of venturing further into the jungle," Sunderland told him. "We would have found you a whole lot quicker."

"I'm sorry. Sorry," the jackeroo moaned, appalled now at his own foolhardiness. "What a savage place this is. Paradise until you step off the track."

"Remember it next time you fell like pulling another daredevil stunt." Sunderland told him bluntly. "Joe and I won't have the time to come after you. You'll have to find your own way home." Sunderland raked a hand through his hair, looked up at the sky. "Let's move on," he sighed, listening carefully to something crashing through the undergrowth. A wild boar? "You can rest up this morning, Rankin. Back to work this afternoon. That's if you want to hold onto your job."

The jackeroo tried desperately to get a grip on himself. To date he had never found anyone better. Action. Adventure. A fantastic guy for a boss. A real life Indiana Jones. Sunderland never showed fear not even in the middle of a stampede that could well have been Ben's fault though no one blamed him. Well maybe Pete Lowell, the overseer. Not too many chances left he thought, his heart quaking. "Yes, sir. Thank you, sir," he muttered. The last thing he wanted was for Sunderland to get rid of him. All the same it had been terrifying his endless hours all alone in the jungle. The ominous weight of the *silence* that was somehow filled with *sound*. He had actually *felt* the presence of the *mimi* spirits greatly feared by the aboriginals in this part of the world. Not that he was ever going to tell anyone about his brush with psychic terror. It had seemed so real. All that whispering and gibbering, ghostly fingers on his cheek. He would never be such a fool again. He just hoped Sunderland would never find out about the bet he'd had with his fellow jackeroo Chris Pearce.

"Want me to drive, boss?" Joe asked quietly, as always looking out for the splendid young man he had watched grow to manhood.

Sunderland shook his head. "Grab forty winks if you can, Joe," he advised, slinging his lean powerful frame behind the wheel. "It's going to be one helluva day and I have an appointment in Darwin tonight."

"The photographer guy? Big shot."

"That's the one. A showing of his work. I've actually seen some at a gallery in Cairns. Wonderful stuff. Very impressive and very expensive. The asking price for many of the prints was thousands. He was getting it too. Photography is supposedly so easy especially these days but I've never seen images quite so extraordinary or insightful. It must have been difficult trying to get the photographs he did. Difficult and dangerous in untouched parts of the world, waiting around for the precise time and conditions, hoping the weather will stay fine."

"So what's he want to do now? The Top End?"

"Why not? The Top End is undoubtedly the most exotic part of Australia. It is even to other Australians a remote and wild world, frontier country, a stepping stone away from Asia. The Territory is the place to wonder at the marvels of nature. Kakadu alone would keep him busy. It's a world heritage area, of international significance as are the cultural artworks of your people, Joe. I don't know if he wants to get down to the Red Centre, Uluru, Kata Tjuta and the Alice but if it's the whole Territory he intends to cover then the Wild Heart is on his itinerary.'

"Nobody could be that good they'd capture *my* country," Joe Goolatta said, fiercely proud and protective of his heritage.

"I guess you're right, Joe," Sunderland said.

They swept across the rugged terrain the jeep bouncing over the rough tracks heading towards North Star homestead. The first streaks of light lay along the horizon, lemon, pink and indigo prefacing dawn. Soon the little Spinifex doves would start to call to one another, music from thousands of tiny throats and the great flights of birds would take to the skies.

"Think you'll help him out?" Joe asked, after a pause of some ten minutes. He was leaning his head, covered in the snow white curls that contrasted so starkly with his skin, against the headrest. He was bone tired, but well into his sixties he was still hard at it.

"Don't know yet," Sunderland muttered, still toying with the idea. "His first choice for a guide was Cy." Sunderland referred to his good friend Cyrus Bannerman of Mokhani Station. "But Cy is still in the honeymoon phase. He can't bear to be away from his Jessica. Can't say I blame him." He saluted his friend's choice. "It was Cy who suggested me."

"Couldn't be anyone better," Joe grunted. "However good Cy is and he *is* I reckon you're even better."

"Prejudiced, Joe." A beam from the head lights picked up a pair of kangaroos who shot up abruptly from behind a grassy mound, turning curious faces. Sunderland swerved to avoid them muttering a mild curse. Kangaroos knew nothing about road rules.

"Thing is whether *you've* got the time," Joe said, totally unable to fall asleep like the kid in the back who was snoring so loudly he wished he had ear plugs.

"If I did go I'd take you with me," Sunderland said glancing at his old friend and childhood mentor.

"Yah kiddin'?" Joe sat up straight, an expression of surprise on his dignified face.

"Who else will take care of me?" Sunderland asked.

Joe's big white grin showed his delight. "I was afraid you might be thinkin' I'm getting too old."

"Never!" Sunderland dropped down a gear for a few hundred metres. "You're better on your feet than a seventeen-year-old. Besides, no one knows this ancient land like you do, Joe. Your people are the custodians of all this."

"Didn't I teach you all I know?" Joe asked gently, thrilled their friendship was so deep.

"It would take a dozen lifetimes," Sunderland said, his eyes on a flight of magpie geese winging from one lagoon to another. "But we're learning. This land was hostile to *my* people when we first came here. Sunderlands came to the wild bush but managed to survive. As cattle men we recognize the debt we owe your people. North Star has always relied on its aboriginal stockmen, bush men and trackers. Elders like you, Joe, have skills we're still learning. I only half know what you do and I'm quite happy to admit it. In the beginning my people feared this land as much as it drew us. Now we love it increasingly in the way you do. We draw closer and closer with every generation. There's no question we all occupy a sacred landscape."

"That we do," Joe answered, deeply moved. "So you think you *could* go then?" Now that he knew he might accompany the young man he worshipped he was excited by the idea.

Sunderland's smile slipped. "I'm a bit worried about leaving Belle at home. She's had a rotten time of it. I can't just abandon her, even if it's only for a couple of weeks."

"Take her along," Joe urged. "Miss Isabelle is as good in the bush as anyone I've seen. She could be an asset."

Sunderland shook his dark head. "I don't see Belle laughing and happy any more, Joe. Neither do you. I know your heart aches for her as well. My sister is a woman who feels very deeply. It'll take her a long time to get over Blair's death. She's punishing herself because his family, his mother in particular, appeared to blame her for his fatal accident."

"Cruel, cruel woman," Joe said. "I disliked that woman from day one." He stopped short of saying he hadn't taken to Miss Isabelle's husband either. Good-looking guy—nothing beside Miss Isabelle's splendid big brother—but as big a snob as his mother—aboriginal man too primitive to look at much less to speak to. No, Joe hadn't taken to Miss Isabelle's dead husband who had died in a car crash after some big society party. Miss Isabelle should have been with him but the awful truth was they had had a well publicised argument at the party before Blair Hartmann had stormed out to his death.

"Dad and I never took to her either," Sunderland sighed. "Incredibly pretentious woman. But Blair was Belle's choice. You know what she was like. As headstrong as they come. Blair was such a change from most guys she knew. A smooth sophisticated *city* guy, high flyer, establishment family, glamorous life style, family mansion on Sydney Harbour."

"Dazzled her for a while," Joe grunted. "But that wasn't really Miss Isabelle."

"No," Sunderland agreed with a heavy heart. "I expect she was acting out a fantasy. She was too young and inexperienced and he was crazy about her. So crazy he practically railroaded her into it. I somehow think she'd never choose someone like Blair Hartmann again though she won't hear a word against him. I don't think I could convince her to go although I know she can handle herself. Hell she was born to it but on principle I don't like women along on those kind of trips. Most of them are trouble. They can't handle the rough. They put themselves and consequently others at risk. It makes it harder for the men."

It took another few minutes before he came out with what was really bothering him. "If Langdon suggests his sister comes along I'm walking."

"Langdon? That's the photographer right? And the sister was the bridesmaid at Cy Bannerman's wedding?" Joe flashed him a shrewd glance. Joe had never met the young lady but unlike everyone else Joe found it easy to read the man he had known from infancy. "I thought you took a real shine to her?" He chuckled and stretched but Sunderland refused to bite.

"How would *you* know?"

"I know." Joe smiled.

"Pretty weird the way you read my mind. You're a sorcerer, Joe Goolatta."

Joe nodded. "Been one in my time."

"Think I don't know that."

Joe closed his eyes.

The memory was seared into his brain like a brand.

The first time he laid eyes on Samantha Langdon she was running down the divided staircase at Mokhani homestead one hand holding up the glistening satin folds of the bridesmaid dress she had just tried on. He and Cy had picked that precise moment to walk in the front door after a long back breaking day. He'd been helping Cy out with a difficult muster, riding shot gun from the helicopter to frighten a stubborn herd of cleanskins out of the heavy scrub. That's what friends were for. He and Cy went back to the toddler stage. He was Cy's best man. Cy would be his if he ever got around to getting married. The floating apparition—that was the only way he could describe her—was a close friend of Cy's bride to be, Jessica, a beautiful young woman, clever, funny with something *real* to say. Samantha Langdon was the chief bridesmaid. One of four. They were to have a rehearsal later on after the men had washed up and had time to catch a cold beer…

The vision laughed, spoke, the words tumbling out as if she were unable to help herself.

"Oh goodness, we didn't think you'd be back so soon!"

She spoke the words at Cy, but rather looked at *him* as though he possessed some kind of uncommon magnetism. He remembered he just stood there, in turn, mesmerized. In the space of a few seconds he was overcome by feelings he had never experienced before. Hot, hard, fierce. They swirled around him like plumes of smoke. The sweat on his body sizzled his skin. It wasn't just her beauty, so bright he felt he had to shield his eyes; it was the way she *moved*. Grace appropriate to a princess and something more. Something that arrested the eye. He supposed ballerinas had it. He wanted to reach for this gilded creature. Close his arms around her. Find her mouth, discover the nectar within.

Then all at once he pulled himself together, regaining his habitual tight control, shocked and wary at her impact. Lightning strikes didn't feature in his emotional life. Why would they? He knew what sorrow a man's obsession bred. He couldn't trust a creature as fascinating as this. The lovely laugh. The teasing voice. The grace and femininity she used to marvellous effect. Not after what had happened to his family. He and Belle had been devastated by their parents' divorce. Their much loved and revered father had never recovered. The wrong woman could destroy a man. He had long assured himself it would never happen to him.

The vision came towards them in her lovely luminous gown, the power to captivate men probably born in her, a creature of air and fire. Her shoulders were bare, her hair a glorious shade of copper streamed down her back. She had beautiful creamy skin, the high cheekbones tinted with apricot almost the colour of her heavy satin gown. He had to tear his eyes away from the slope of her breasts revealed above the low cut bodice. This was a powerful sexual encounter. Nothing more.

"It's Ross, isn't it?"

Not content to hold him spellbound her charm and breeding was about to reduce him to an oaf.

Cy smiling, started to introduce them with his engaging manner. He on the other hand must have appeared an ill mannered boor by contrast, stiff and standoffish. A consequence he knew of his strong reaction A man could drown in a woman's eyes. Large, meltingly soft velvety brown eyes with gold chips in the iris. He knew the colour in her cheeks deepened when he looked down at her. *Stared* probably, not doing a good job of covering his innate hostility. He remembered he made some excuse about not taking her hand, standing well back so the dust and grime off his work gear wouldn't come into contact with her beautiful gown. He knew he looked and felt like a savage. He found out later there was a dried smear of blood on his cheek bone.

She had endured his severity well. Right through that evening and the great day of the wedding. It was all so damned disturbing. He wasn't usually like that. Looking back on his behaviour he cringed, cursing himself for his own susceptibility. It was a weakness and it pricked his pride. Maybe the Sunderlands weren't fated to have happy emotional lives. His dad, then Belle. The very last thing he needed was to be enslaved by a woman. The secret he was convinced was never to lose sight of himself.

"Hey, where dja go?"

Joe's voice broke into his troubled reverie, sounding a little worried.

"Just thinking."

"About that girl?" Joe studied the strong profile in the increasing light.

"About Belle." He had no trouble lying.

Joe took it Ross didn't want to talk about it. "Hell, man, better Miss Isabelle don't mope about the homestead," he said. "Is she gunna go with you tonight?"

Sunderland shrugged as if to say he wasn't sure. "My sister at the great age of twenty-six has reached a crisis point in life. I'm just grateful she chose to come home. It was bad enough losing Dad the way we did. Two years later Belle loses her husband."

Joe wondered as much as anyone else what exactly that last argument between husband and wife had been about. Miss

Isabelle hadn't just been grieving when she returned to the Sunderland ancestral home. She was and remained in a deep depression which led Joe to remembering what a glorious young creature she had been. The apple of her father's eye, Ross his great pride. The Sunderlands had become a very close family after the children's mother, Diana, who had been a wonderful wife and mother to start with fell in love with some guy she met on a visit to relatives in England. In fact a distant cousin. Within a month Diana had decided he meant more to her than her husband back home in Australia. She'd had high hopes of gaining custody of her children but they had refused to leave their father. Ewan Sunderland was a wonderful, generous, caring man. An ideal husband and father. He had idolised his beautiful wife. Put her on a pedestal. At least it had taken her all of fourteen years to fall off, Joe thought sadly. Such a beautiful woman! She laughed a lot. So happy! Always bright and positive. Wonderful to his people. Then all of a sudden put under a powerful spell. Love magic. Only this time it was *black magic*.

All these years later Joe's eyes grew wet. Her defection had severed Ewan's heart strings. The children had suffered. Three years apart. Ross, twelve, Isabelle only nine. Joe still couldn't fathom how Diana had done it. The cruelty of it! Now Ewan Sunderland lay at peace struck down by a station vehicle that got out of control. A bizarre double tragedy because the driver, a long time employee had died as well, a victim of a massive heart attack at the wheel. The shock had been enormous and none of them had really moved on. Ewan Sunderland was sorely missed by his son and daughter and his legion of friends.

Isabelle woke with a start. For a moment she couldn't remember where she was. The room was dark. There was no sound. Her heart hammering she put out a hand and slid it across the sheet. Nothing. No one. A stream of relief poured through her.

Thank God! She pressed her dark head woven into a loose plait back into the pillow, her feeling of disorientation slowly evaporating. She lay there a few minutes longer fighting off the effects of her dreams, so vivid, so deeply disturbing she felt like crying. The same old nightmares really. She could feel the familiar fingers of depression starting to tighten their grip on her, but she knew she had to fight it. No one could cure her but herself. There were still people who loved her—her brother most of all—but she had to solve her problems on her own. Another approach might have been to talk to a psychologist trained to deal with women's "problems" but she was never *never* going to tell anyone what her married life had been like. The truth was too shocking.

Her bedroom was growing lighter, brighter. Soon the birds would start their dawn symphony. Did those wonderful birds know how much emotional support they gave her. The beauty and power of their singing cut a path through her negative feelings, the grief, the anger, the guilt and at bottom the disgust she directed at herself.

Determinedly she threw back the light coverlet and slid out of bed her bare toes curling over the Persian rug. A glance at the bedside clock confirmed what she had guessed: 4:40.

Oh God! So early, but there was no way she could go back to sleep. In her dreams Blair slept with her, a hand of possession on her breast. That's what she had been to him. A possession. Some kind of prize. He put a high value on her. Her looks and her manner. He had even insisted on coming with her to buy her clothes. Only the best would do. Roaming around her, viewing back and front, giving his opinion while the saleswoman beamed at him, no doubt fantasizing what life would be like with a rich handsome loving husband like that.

If only they knew!

Fully awake now, she tried to shrug off the memory of Blair's voice. It still had the power to resound in her ears. So tender and loving, so full of desire. That alone had filled her with trepidation. Then as predictably as night followed day, full of a white hot fury and the queerest anguish, berating her. His hand against her throat while she froze in paralysis.

You make me do this. You just don't understand, do you? What it's like for me. You cold neurotic bitch! What have I got to do to make you love me? What, Isabelle, tell me. I can't put up with any more of your cruelty. You will understand, won't you? I'll make you!

Then a blow that made her double over. Who could have dreamed such a charming young man could be capable of such behaviour? Cushioned in normality, the love of her father and brother and then Blair. In a single day everything changed.

What have I got to do, Belle, to make you love me? For all the very public displays of loving and remarked generosity Blair was what her grandmother would have called "a home devil." Correction. Blair *had been* a home devil. Blair was dead and a lot of people blamed her. Probably they always would. Certainly his family, especially his mother, Evelyn, who had bitterly resented being ousted as the number one woman in her only son's life. But then, she was to blame. How could anyone think otherwise? Maybe things in her own past—her mother's destruction of a marriage and the childhood trauma she had suffered had played a part in the calamity of Blair's death. Maybe her mother had passed on her destructive genes to her? This feeling was especially strong in her. A sense of guilt. Yet it could be argued she was being very unfair to herself. She used to be such a positive person. Not now. Being with Blair had poisoned her. She had never told a soul of his psychological cruelties, the little mind games, much less the unpredictable rages when he had resorted to physical blows, trying to pummel her until she found the courage to fight back. Sometimes it happened he came off second best. She reminded herself she was a Sunderland. She told him it had to stop. It was so *demeaning*. She wouldn't tolerate it. She would leave him.

No joke, Blair, she told him when he began to laugh, swinging around on him, picking up a knife. *No joke!*

Something in her eyes must have warned him she was in deadly earnest. After the confrontations, the usual deluge of apologies. Van loads of red roses. Exquisite underwear and nightgowns he loved to tear off. Blair down on his knees begging her to forgive him. He idolised her. She was everything in the world to him. He despised himself when he lost his temper. *Hated* what he did to her. But didn't she realise it was *her* fault she made him so angry? She deliberately provoked him, always trying to score points like a skilled opponent with an inexperienced adversary. It hurt him desperately the way she flirted with other men. People talked about it.

How could they? She never did...

And why did she have to go on about a *baby* for God's sake? Wasn't he enough for her? She had already stopped talking about a baby. Honest with no one else—her damnable pride again, her blind refusal to admit she had made a terrible mistake—she was honest with *herself*. The days of her marriage were numbered. Almost three years on, she wondered how she had married Blair in the first place.

Well, she had paid the price. Far better that they had never come into one another's lives. She knew Ross thought she had been in deep mourning these past months. Well she had in a sense. Mourning the waste of a life. What might have been. It was her failure to be able to mourn Blair's removal from her life that was the problem. She hadn't deserved his treatment of her—no woman did—but she did deserve her crushing feelings of guilt. It was what she had said to Blair that last night of his life that had sent him on his no return journey to death.

Isabelle showered and dressed then went downstairs to prepare breakfast for her brother. The best brother in the world. She loved him dearly. When she thought about it they had never had a single fight right through their childhood and adolescence which wasn't the norm in a lot of households. Ross's aim had been to love and protect her just as it had been their father's. Both men in her life had tried their hardest to make up for the painful loss of a mother. They couldn't bear to see her cry and after a while she had stopped. She was a Sunderland.

So many losses she thought. Mother, father, husband. Losses aplenty. Plenty of bad memories. Plenty of scars.

She heard Ross come in and moved into the hall to greet him, wiping her hands on a tea towel. "Find the boy?"

He nodded. "I don't think he'll pull that stunt again. Had some bet with young Pearce he could make it back to camp on his own. The only thing is he headed in the wrong direction."

"Easy enough to do if you're stupid." Isabelle gave a half smile. "Ready for breakfast?"

"In about ten minutes okay?" Ross needed a shave and a shower. Out all night he showed no signs of strain or tiredness. "You don't have to get up this early, you know," he turned back to tell his sister gently.

"My sleeping habits aren't what they used to be," Isabelle answered. In truth she was immensely grateful to sleep alone.

Her brother heard the sorrow behind the words and misconstrued it.

Isabelle let him make inroads on a substantial breakfast, sausages, bacon, eggs, tomatoes a couple of hash browns, toast, before starting any conversation. She smiled at the enthusiasm with which he attacked his meal. She couldn't fill him. Never could. A big man like their dad. Six three, whip-cord lean with a wide wedge of shoulders. His down bent head gleamed blue black like her own. His fine grained skin was a dark gold. His eyes like hers were a remarkable aqua. Their mother's eyes. Otherwise they were Sunderlands through and through. When they were just little kids people had often mistaken them for twins, but Ross grew and grew while she stopped at five-eight, above average height for a woman.

"So have you made up your mind about tonight?" She

poured them both a cup of really good coffee—a must—hot, black and strong the way they liked it. None of that milky stuff.

He didn't answer for a moment, absently chewing a piece of toast. "I don't know."

"Hey, they're expecting you," she reminded him, knowing full well he didn't like to leave her. "Cy and Jessica will be there. After all, Jessica was the one who arranged it all. It's Robyn's gallery." Robyn was Cy's rather difficult stepsister married to a big developer. "You'll see Samantha again."

His lean handsome features tautened. "Who said I wanted to?"

"Sorry. I don't mean to pry." Isabelle considered for a moment. "She got under your skin didn't she?"

"Yes," he said bluntly. "I don't like women getting under my skin."

It was no revelation to his sister. "We've paid heavily for our past, haven't we?"

"Sure have." His eyes reflected the grimness of his thoughts. "The past can spoil relationships."

"I know. It's all patterned and planned and destined." He looked at her. Always slender Belle was close to fragile. There were shadows under her eyes from many hours of lost sleep and probably bad dreams but she was indisputably *beautiful*. That was the main reason Hartmann had wanted her. For her beauty. It had woven a spell around him. With so many other things about Belle to appreciate and admire, her intelligence, her talent, her sheer *quality* Hartmann had seemed to ignore all that. If indeed he even saw it. Poor Belle! She had rushed in to a marriage that probably wouldn't have endured even if Blair had lived.

"Talk to me, Belle," he found himself pleading. "I'm here to listen. Tell me what went so terribly wrong in your marriage?"

"I'm a tough nut like you. I keep it all locked up." Isabelle stirred a few more grains of raw sugar into her coffee.

"It might help to talk don't you think?"

What could she say? Good-looking, softly spoken, Blair had been abusive? What an upsurge of rage that would arouse!

It was *unthinkable* to tell her brother, just as she had never been able to tell her father. It was all *so* demeaning. Both Sunderlands big strong *tough* men living a life fraught with dangers and non stop physically exhausting work, would have cut off a hand before lifting it in anger to a woman. Her father had never so much as given her a light slap even when she got up to lots of mischief. Ross was intensely chivalrous. An old word but it applied to him and a great many Outback men who cherished women as life's partners and close friends. Blair could have considered himself done for if she had ever told her father or brother of her treatment at his hands. But for all his insecurities, cunning Blair had known she would never expose him. In exposing him she would be devaluing herself. Pride, too, was a sin. There was just no way she could tell her brother her terrible story. He would wonder if she had been in her right mind not seeking her family's protection.

"Well?" Ross prompted after a few moments of watching the painful expressions flit across his sister's face. "He adored you, didn't he? I mean he was *really* mad about you. It might seem strange but Dad and I never thought he plumbed the *real* you. Was that it? Terrible to speak ill of the dead and the tragic way he died so young, but Blair gave the impression he was extraordinarily dependent on you. Needy I suppose is the word. You couldn't walk out of the room ten minutes before he was asking where you were. Who you were with. You don't have to tell me but I know he was terribly jealous. Even of our family bond. Did it become a burden?"

She couldn't meet her brother's eyes. "We had problems, Ross." She concentrated on the bottom of her coffee cup. "I imagine most married couples do, but we were trying to work them out."

"What problems?" Ross persisted, knowing there was a great deal his sister wasn't telling." I know you wanted to start a family. You love children. Every woman wishes for a baby with the man she loves."

*Only I didn't love him. Blair was the baby. Blair wanted a
real baby to stay away. His mania was her sole attention.*

"There's no point in talking about it now, Ross," she sighed.
"I feel terrible Blair had to die the way he did. Such a waste of
a life!"

His brows drew together in a frown. "Surely you mean you
find it unbearable to be without him?"

"Of course. We both know what it's like to lose someone
we love."

"But you can't despair, Belle. You're young. In time you'll
meet someone else." Someone *worthy* of you, Ross thought. "I
realise the fact the two of you had an argument before Blair left
the party is weighing heavily on you. His mother's attitude
didn't help but she was so intensely possessive of her son she
would have blamed any woman who was his widow. Grief
made her act so badly."

*By and large Evelyn Hartmann was right. She had sent Blair
to his death.*

"Evelyn wasn't the only one to assign the blame to me.
Blair's whole family did. A lot of our so called friends looked
at me differently afterwards. There was a lot of talk. I couldn't
defend myself. I was the *outsider*. Everyone looked on Blair
as the most devoted of husbands."

"But *wasn't* he?" Ross asked, hoping he could get to the
truth. Did the truth set you free or make matters worse?

"He adored me just as you say, Ross." Isabelle spread her elegant long fingered hands. "I know you're trying to help me but
can we get off the subject." *Stay away from it entirely.* "Samatha
Langdon now. I'd like to meet her. I missed out on Cy's and
Jessica's wedding. Impossible to go under the circumstances."

"Cy and Jessica understood," Ross assured her. "If you really want to meet Samantha Langdon why not come along with
me tonight? We'll take the chopper into Darwin late afternoon.
You'll need to book an extra room at the hotel. I think it might
do you good to get out of the house."

Would it? All the hurtful rumours and she supposed she hadn't heard the half of them had given her a strong feeling of being *separated* from other people. Her problem—early widowhood and ugly spate of rumours—wasn't *their* problem, thank God. She knew all the gossip would be doing the rounds of Darwin but then she wouldn't be on her own. Nevertheless she said: "It's just that I don't think I can, Ross." She began to gather up plates remembering how Blair in one of his moods had smashed their wine glasses, deliberately dropping them on the kitchen tiles, then laughing as she shrunk back wondering seriously if he were mad. Certainly there had been a demon in him.

"Look Belle, I'm not pressing you but I know there's a heck of a lot you're not telling me. Just remember, you're not alone. A lot of people love you. You're my baby sister. I'd lay down my life for you."

Tears rushed into her eyes and she turned away.

"So it would mean a great deal to me if you made the effort to come. Jessica likes you a lot."

Isabelle had composed herself enough to turn back. "We've only met a couple of times but Jessica is a lovely person and Samantha is a close friend. Would Jessica have a friend who wasn't a nice person?"

Ross stood up, shoving his chair beneath the table. "I never said she wasn't *nice*." God, nice hardly described her. "It's David Langdon we're there to meet anyway. Say you'll come, Belle."

"You need protection?" She gave a glimmer of a smile.

"Nope." He moved his wide shoulders restlessly. "Getting hooked on a woman like that would be as dangerous as catching a tiger by the tail."

CHAPTER TWO

THEY slipped into an animated crowd, most with champagne glasses in hand, and waiters circling with delicious looking finger food. There was a buzz of a hundred voices. Isabelle spotted Cyrus Bannerman first because of his commanding height and presence. Half hidden by the breadth of his shoulder was his beautiful wife of several months Jessica, her magnificent mass of ash-blond hair radiant in the bright fall of skylights. The interior of the gallery was divided into three spacious rooms interconnected by wide arches. The lights were trained on a large collection of photographs, most colour some black and white that took on a rivetting quality to rival paintings. Someone had taken the trouble to hang the prints *perfectly* on the white expanse of walls.

Jessica looked up and waved, a lovely welcoming smile on her face. Cy turned around to follow his wife's gaze, beaming too. They watched him glance back at the group he was with, obviously making their excuses, before he tucked his hand beneath Jessica's elbow steering a path towards Ross and Isabelle who were also being greeted on all sides. The big cattle families were outback royalty. The Sunderlands were as well known as the Bannermans though the late Broderick Bannerman, an immensely wealthy man had not scored anywhere near the late Ewan Sunderland's high approval rating. Mercifully both sons and heirs were held in high regard.

"Hi!" The women brushed cheeks, smiling into one another's eyes. The men, looking very pleased to see one another settled for affectionate claps on the shoulder.

"I'm so glad you could come, Isabelle," Jessica said with complete sincerity. "You look absolutely beautiful."

"Thank you. So do you." Isabelle, who appeared so poised was actually quaking inside. She was grateful for the compliment. Jessica's warmth and friendliness steadied her. It was a long time since she had ventured out. Blair's death had put such a contagion on her.

Jessica smiled. "It's a brilliant collection." She turned her head over her shoulder. "I know you'll both love it. David is being feted in the next room. Sam is with David's assistant, Matt Howarth. A very pleasant guy. Come and meet them. David is an extraordinary man. You'll like him, Ross. We know he's very keen on meeting you and hopefully having you for a guide."

"Piece of cake!" Cy assured his friend.

"I don't know that I've made up my mind, Cy," Ross said, sobering a moment. *Sam was with Matt Howarth?* What did that mean? What do you think it means he thought a hard knot in his stomach.

"You want a break. You work too hard," Cy urged him, forging a path through the throng.

"*You* should talk."

"It's not like it's going to be for long. Belle would *love* it." The *old* Belle, Cy thought. Knowing her from childhood he recognised and understood Isabelle's fragile state of mind.

Jessica made a little surprised gesture, looking towards Isabelle. "What a marvellous idea!"

"I couldn't, Jessica," Isabelle said quickly, touching the other woman's arm. "I beg you, don't say anything."

"Of course not!" Jessica promised hurriedly seeing the tension in Isabelle's face. She knew Isabelle's tragic story and she was full of sympathy. How did a woman cope with losing a beloved husband? Jessica found herself giving an involuntary shudder. Her own days were filled with ecstatic fulfilment. To lose Cy would be like a descent into hell.

Someone came out of the crowd, a stylish, sweet faced woman in her fifties who grasped Isabelle's arm. "Isabelle dear, what an extraordinary surprise! I'd heard you were home."

"Mrs. Charlton, of course." Isabelle's face lit up. She allowed herself to be detained. "I'll catch up with you," she called to the others.

Ross relaxed when he heard the comfortable note in his sister's voice. He didn't know the woman, although he was sure he had seen her some place. So many of Isabelle's so called friends had betrayed her taking the opinion she somehow had played a role in her popular husband's death.

The next room was even more crowded. A lion of a man with a large handsome head covered in thick tawny waves and strongly hewn features was holding court. The several women around him were staring up into his face, magnetised, their expressions buoyed up, obviously excited.

Jessica laughed a bit, "Starstruck."

"Extraordinary guy," Cy answered. In fact very few in life had that impact he thought.

But Ross saw no one but *her*. The same galvanising jolt passed through him as the first time he'd laid eyes on her. A sensation he had tried—how unsuccessfully—to erase from his mind. And then, tensing, the man standing too close at her shoulder. Early thirties, slight of build, thin sensitive face, nice smile. Matt Howarth. It had to be. His attitude, the way he was standing flashed an unmistakable message. They shared a relationship, or at the very least an understanding. Surely he hadn't imagined she would be unattached. A beautiful creature like that! Hell he couldn't even allow himself to think of her, but the knowledge he wouldn't succeed was there.

Tonight she was wearing a slip of a dress of a golden hue that complemented her colouring. High heeled gold sandals were on her feet. Her beautiful hair was centre parted falling like a bolt of bright copper satin down her back. Even her skin looked gilded. He could actually feel its smoothness under his hand. Cool and satiny when the very thought of touching her heated his blood.

You want her. You know you do.

He heard that inner voice, the voice that wouldn't be silenced, whispering in his ear.

Their eyes met. He realised with a sense of crushing mortification he'd been standing once *again* transfixed. *Hell!* Acting foolish wasn't his style. He found himself wondering if the others had noticed he was rooted to the spot. Yet she too, seemed shocked, her beautiful doe's eyes widening, as if electrified by the intensity of his hunter's gaze.

Immediately he was seized with the fierce desire to turn around and leave. This woman was temptation. The sort of challenge any smart man would step free of it. No way could he guide this expedition if Samantha Langdon was to go along. He hadn't the slightest desire to allow a woman to play him like a clown. Woman magic. Sometimes he thought he could never wipe away the bitter taste of his father's betrayal at the soft hands of his mother. That's what lay behind everything he thought, abruptly sobering. A man could be shackled by adoration. His beloved father had gone about his life but both of his children had known inside he was shattered. That's what women were capable of. Leaving a trail of destruction.

He looked away at the brother, David Langdon, thinking with a vague sense of astonishment he liked the man on sight. Brother and sister shared a resemblance—not as marked as his and Belle's—mostly the colouring. She looked very delicate beside him, ultra feminine. Long, light beautiful bones. The brother was a big man, well over six feet like himself, but strapping rather than lean, very fit and strong looking. His hair was a tawny mix of dark blond to bronze, his eyes a pronounced shade of topaz. Both had generous well defined mobile mouths.

Cy introduced them. The two men shook hands then Langdon speaking easily—he exuded charisma—introduced his assistant, Matt, who regarded Sunderland somewhat warily as if he thought this was someone who could turn dangerous and he was already aware of it.

"I'm looking forward to us all having dinner together," Langdon said after a few minutes of exchanging social pleasantries. "Meanwhile I hope you enjoy the showing. I have to circulate, it seems." Cy's stepsister, Robyn, the owner of the gallery, looking very glamorous in black and white was beckoning to him pushing forward a distinguished looking elderly man. "Excuse me, won't you?" Langdon's manner was so warm and charming Ross thought the man would have no difficulty selling heaters to the nomads in the desert. David Langdon had every appearance of a man you could trust with your life.

They all began to study the remarkable array of photographs, moving about the room in procession. Ross listened to the comments of his friends as they talked. Jessica, the creative one, was very knowledgeable. She was just right for Cy he thought. Lucky guy! He wondered where Belle had got to. Ah, there she was, standing with a red-haired woman, seemingly at ease. He stopped for a moment to read a CV of Langdon's work. Very impressive. He'd spent time in the war zones, East Timor, Afghanistan, Iraq. He was very widely travelled. A great deal in South East Asia. Thailand, Cambodia, Indonesia, Malaysia, Papua New Guinea. Ross had seen his marvellous impressions of that little known country although it lay on Australia's door step. Separated momentarily from the others—so many people wanted to meet Jessica—he studied the shots of the Great Barrier Reef and the glorious tropical islands. Langdon must have spent hours and hours flying around trying to find the exact spots. Probably in a helicopter or a light plane, door open, strapped in tightly so he could film. Perfect crystal clear waters, cobalt skies, pure white sand ringing jade islands.

He wouldn't mind a few weeks on a tropical island. He could almost feel himself there. His eyes dwelt with pleasure on a magnificent shot of the Outer Reef shot from the air. The deep channel was a deep inky blue, the waters a deep turquoise, with channels of aquamarine. The fantastic coral gardens were in the foreground, an anchored boat and a group of snorkellers swimming off the reef wall lending perspective. Moving on, he recognised Four Mile Beach at Queensland's Port Douglas, the purple ranges in the background, luxuriant palms and vegetation wrapping the wide beach, sun worshippers like little colourful dots on the sand. A marvellous, marvellous shot of a small sand cay covered with nesting crested terns, the deep turquoise waters rippled with iridescent green like the heart of a black opal. He felt like he was in the middle of the ocean.

"These are good," he found himself murmuring aloud.

"You sound surprised?"

He straightened and turned slowly before answering, giving himself time to suppress the involuntary electric thrill that flared along his nerves. As a consequence his voice came out in that strange arrogant fashion. "That wasn't my intention. Your brother is more than a fine photographer. He's an artist."

"He is," Samantha said with complete conviction, her cheeks flushing a little at the curtness of his tone. Her powerful attraction to this man shocked her. Not Mr. Nice Guy that's for sure. Formidable. "I run the Sydney gallery for him. Of course you know that. We're thinking of opening another one here in Darwin."

"And what do you suppose Robyn will think about that?" Incredibly in his imagination he was pushing her low necked dress down from her shoulders. She had beautiful breasts. She had teased him with their beauty at the wedding, smiling into his eyes, provoking him to dance with her. Of course he was obliged to. They were after all chief bridesmaid and best man.

She was shrugging lightly as if to show she was unfazed by his scrutiny and the challenge of his comment. "There's plenty of room for another gallery. Robyn specialises in paintings and sometimes sculptures. Hopefully one gallery will be a spin off for the other. There are always a great many tourists in town."

"Yes," he agreed briefly, feeling as though he was drunk on some rich potent wine. That was the effect she had on him. But no way, *no way,* was he about to fall to his knees.

She was returning his gaze equably, so gracious when he always acted the complete boor around her. He suspected she was doing it deliberately.

"I'm wondering why you don't like me, Ross?" she inquired softly. "No, don't throw up your head." Which he did in that high mettled way. "Don't deny it. We both know it's true. Remember how it was at the wedding?"

As if he had forgotten.

"I didn't imagine your…what can I call it? Animus, antagonism? Was it something I said? Something I did? I seem to have gone over it many many times in my head. But it's still there tonight. The thing is, David and I are so hoping you'll act as our guide. It would be awkward if there remained *difficulties* between us."

He frowned, giving her a look that both smouldered and sparkled. "You intend to go along then?"

"I've never seen a man with aquamarine eyes." She was so unnerved she didn't answer his question, but said the first thing that came into her head.

"It runs in the family." He returned carelessly. "Lest you deflect me, I'll ask again. Do you intend to go along on this trip?"

There was no mistaking the opposition on his hard, handsome face. "I'm thrilled David wants me," she said, feeling the friction between them like a burr against the skin. "I don't know if you've noticed the little texts beneath the photographs. I was responsible for them."

It was a reflex to compliment her. He had thought they were Langdon's; a few lines, often poetic capturing the very essence of the scene. "Very good."

"I don't think you know—I made such a poor impression on you at Cy's and Jessica's wedding but I write and illustrate children's stories as well as managing the gallery. They're for children with vivid imaginations. They're starting to do very well. Jessica and I took a Fine Arts Degree together, but I'm not nearly so gifted as she. It won't be too long before Jessica gives an exhibition of her paintings. She not only fell madly in love with her Territory Man, she fell in love with the Territory. So far David hasn't photographed the Top End or the Red Centre which has been widely covered of course. He likes to capture his subject matter in a new light."

"And it works." He tried hard to lighten up but that was difficult when he was standing less than an arm's length from her. "You realise a trip into Kakadu wouldn't be a picnic?"

She tilted her chin, hoping her eyes weren't betraying her reactions. This man attracted and daunted her in equal measure. "I know it's a great wilderness area."

He nodded, his black hair sheened with purple highlights like the sky at midnight. For a cattle man used to working gear, off duty he was very stylishly groomed. Dark cream linen suit. White shirt with a brown stripe the top button casually undone. Silk tie with alternating white and brown stripes. Sexy enough to take her breath away.

"Have you ever got up close and personal with a twenty foot croc?" he asked with light sarcasm.

"I'd make sure *you* were in front of me." She tried to joke.

"It's no joke," he told her, his lean features taut.

"I'll have you know I'm serious." She looked directly at him, feeling on her mettle. "What is it, Ross? Have you written me off as a bimbo? Someone who'll turn into a quivering liability?"

"I have to tell you I wouldn't be happy to take you," he said bluntly.

"Samantha," she prompted. "That's my name. Sam, if you like."

"*Sam* is just *too* quaint." Anyone less like a Sam he had yet to see. He gazed into her dark doe eyes, bright with little golden motes.

She could have hit him. Damaged her hand. *Herself.* "Actually I was hoping your sister, Isabelle—she's *so* beautiful—might be persuaded to come along with us. Station bred she'd be an enormous help to me."

He could only warn her off. "Belle wouldn't be interested, I'm afraid. She lost her husband not so long ago."

Samantha dipped her head, her nerves tightening. "Jessica told me. I'm so very sorry. She's so young. Mightn't it help her to get out though, don't you think? Nature is a great healer."

Very deliberately he cut off that line of thinking. "Thank you for sharing that with me, *Samantha.*"

The effect of her name on his lips was extraordinary. How strange it was to be excited by a man and thoroughly disconcerted at the same time. "Don't be like that," she pleaded.

"Like what?" He was sizzling with sexual energy. A male aggression that appeared to possess him in her presence. Chaos threatened when he liked order.

"Arrogant, actually," she told him quietly, feeling a twist of desire deep inside her and nothing she could do about it. "Unpleasant as well when Cy thinks you're the greatest guy in the world."

"Maybe I'm a lot more used to dealing with men than women. I'm sorry. I apologise."

His sudden smile made her suck in her breath. It bathed his rather severe handsome features in dazzling light. "That's not what I've heard either," she found herself saying.

"Meaning what?" He shrugged, a surprisingly elegant movement.

"There are a lot of girls hung up on you I was told. I suppose that's a good sign. Then again a lot of women are attracted to men who have little use for them."

"And you're assuming I'm that kind of man?"

The colour of his remarkable eyes was a source of wonder. "Aren't you?" Her every instinct had warned her this man was trouble yet she plunged ahead angered by his resistance, almost dismissal. It wasn't something she was used to.

"I love my sister," he pointed out.

"You certainly should. You had to stick together."

His expression tightened. "Cy told you my life story?"

"What's wrong with that? I was interested. He filled me in a little way. I know your parents divorced when you were twelve and your sister a few years younger. Don't feel overly bad about that. Our mother and father split up when I was still at school and David had already left home. Both of them are re-married. David and I have two stepbrothers—my dad's. Things like that."

He was surprised. He had thought her the most cosseted of creatures. Daddy's little princess. A most beautiful little girl. But there was a sudden haunting in her eyes. "You can't quite cover up the fact you'd been praying they'd stay together?"

"Absolutely, but they'd hit a very bumpy ride. In fact it's put me off marriage."

"True?" He let his smile loose again.

Another thrill. That alone shouted a warning. "I've already decided *you* have a lot against it."

"Really?" He looked down his straight nose at her. "You don't know me." *Even if you are trying to lead me on.*

Her heart gave a wild flutter. She couldn't believe the arrogance of his manner could be a seduction. But it *was*. "I'd like to know you better," she said, something she'd discovered the moment she'd laid eyes on him.

"So you can dig out my weaknesses?" He *willed* his blood to stop racing. There was a tremendous exhilaration in this sparring. It was like being caught up in an electrical storm when at any moment danger could be inflicted on a man.

"I didn't imagine for a moment you had any," she answered with faintly bitter sweetness.

"As many as the next man." He shrugged. "But I work hard to keep them under control. I had the impression you and your brother's assistant were close?"

A flare of something, was it anger? deepened the apricot colour in her cheeks. "Now how on earth did you arrive at that conclusion?"

"Are you telling me it's not true?" Sad if he was giving *himself* away.

"I'm not telling you anything," she said crisply, knowing with every passing minute getting involved with this intoxicating man would be a terrible mistake. "I'd like to see you less sure of yourself and your opinions."

"And you're the one hoping we can be friends?" he scoffed.

Think, Sam. Try to clear your head.

Yet all her pulses were drumming in double time. "Not *friends* so much," she successfully mustered her poise. "I don't believe we could ever be friends, not unless you undergo a radical change, but colleagues of sorts. I know you'd prefer Men Only, women being such nuisances, but I'd endeavour to keep out of your way."

"Fine," he drawled, staring down at her mouth with her small teeth like prize pearls. Her lips were full, luscious, incredibly tempting. He'd like to crush their cushiony softness beneath his. Teach her a lesson. "But not exactly easy if we had to share a tent?"

She battled the shock wave. "We wouldn't have to do that. *Would* we?"

For the first time there was genuine amusement in his jewelled eyes. "Not your idea of fun? It could get worse."

She was still seeing them sharing a tent. "Like dodging crocs and pythons that devour you at a gulp?"

"Lady, there's so much I'm *not* telling you." It came out with a flicker of contempt.

Use your head. Go!

She had to make her escape before she said something she

would regret. Ross Sunderland was dynamite. Exciting yes, but one of the dangerous men of this world. He drew her so much it was scaring her badly. "Anything to put me off," she managed lightly. "I think I'll have a word with Isabelle if I can find her. *You're* a terrible man." She half turned away.

"Knowing that at the start will save you a lot of trouble," he called after her.

"To be frank I knew it the instant I laid eyes on you." She turned back to confront him, long silky hair swirling, flame bright in the strong lights.

His mouth curved in a challenging smile. "Then you know we're not fated to be *friends*."

"That sounds so much like a *dare*?"

They were caught in a tableau, neither moving until a very pretty brunette dressed in show stopping red broke it up by rushing between them, ignoring Samantha as though she weren't there. "Ah there you are Ross, darling!" She grabbed his arm. Held on for dear life. "I didn't think this was your scene. Mum and I have only just arrived. Come and join us. We were just saying we should have a good party. It's seems like *ages* since we got together." She began to pull him away.

Samantha didn't wait to see them move off. She was cursing herself for allowing Ross Sunderland to get to her. No way either was he going to block her path. Her company and contribution were important to her brother. She was determined not to be left behind.

David Langdon took a long slow breath then decided to catch up with the woman he'd spent so much time watching. Albeit out of the corner of his eye. *A beaute fatale.* Of course he had known she was beautiful. In fact she was more beautiful in the flesh than she was in the photographs he had seen in the papers and the few times they had captured her on television always hurrying away, head bent, one hand trying to cover her face like the tragic Princess Diana. For a while the media had hounded her. That must have been a bad experience. He knew who she was of course. Isabelle Hartmann, Blair Hartmann's young widow. She couldn't be more than mid-twenties and her beauty hadn't even reached its zenith. She still looked as though she was hurting badly.

David hadn't even told his sister how much he had learned about this near notorious young woman over the past months. Mostly from people supposedly in the know. Little of it good. It seemed to him a shocking thing to condemn her out of hand. Who knew exactly what went on within a marriage? Closer to the truth he'd been seized with a fierce desire to protect her which was quite odd since he had never managed to meet her. Not that he wasn't in and out of Sydney all the time but he made a point of avoiding the big social functions unless they were in aid of charity. His deep seeing eyes, *trained* eyes, had divined the torment in her.

A lot of the rumours and gossip had their origins in plain jealousy. He'd come to that conclusion. Men he'd found were far more reluctant to put any blame at all on her though all were in agreement Blair Hartmann had been a nice easy going guy, maybe a little light weight, spoiled outrageously by his wealthy mother. Everyone knew that. It was women, especially Evelyn Hartmann's circle, fuelled by envy and resentment and fearing to cross such a formidable figure in society as Isabelle's ex-mother-in-law, who claimed Isabelle was an altogether different person from the one who appeared in public. For one thing she had been near arctic to the husband who had adored her. There was even talk she had refused him a child no doubt to preserve her willowy figure, selfish creature. She was terribly vain they reported, obsessed with herself and her clothes.

At least they couldn't say she had married Hartmann for his money. The Sunderlands were a highly respected pastoral family wealthy in their own right as the press had easily uncovered. The fierce argument between the two, husband and wife had of course found its way into print. Speculation had been rife.

Something Isabelle Hartmann had said had caused her late husband so loving and appreciative of her, to storm out of the party. Worse, perhaps caused him to be careless of his own life.

Whispers still followed her. He had overheard a few this very night. Blessed or cursed by such physical beauty she was bound to be a cynosure of attention. But no one he had noticed had been so careless as to give rein to gossip with her brother in earshot. Ross Sunderland was a man with fire in his remarkable eyes. Even the way he stood near his sister, sometimes with his arm carelessly around her, told the world not to be surprised if he retaliated on his sister's behalf. Langdon had been told and had since witnessed the two were very close. My God, didn't he feel the same about his own little sister, Samantha, nearly seven years his junior who had borne the brunt of their parents' undeniably bitter break up with Sam the pawn in the middle. On his world travels at the time he had since done his level best to make it up to her.

Seeing Isabelle Hartmann alone for a moment that beautiful face cool, passionless as a statue, he made his way towards her, gesturing with a smile he'd get back to a couple who surged across the room to gain his attention.

"Good evening, Mrs. Hartmann. I've been meaning to introduce myself for some time. David Langdon."

She turned to him quickly, staring up into his face. "Of course, Mr. Langdon." Some emotion stirred in her, swiftly crossed her face, then disappeared. She gave him her hand, silky soft, slender quite lost in his bear grip. He fought down the powerful urge to carry it to his lips.

"My pleasure." She smiled, finding something incredibly mesmeric about this big, dynamic man. "And it certainly has been. I've so enjoyed your showing."

"I'm glad." Was it his imagination or was she trembling?

"I'd have met you much earlier only I got caught up by friends who haven't seen me for a while. You've been so much the centre of attention I didn't want to intrude." The fact was both Cy and Jessica, then a little later Samantha followed by Ross had insisted they introduce her—it was high time—but for some reason she had made the excuse she would wait a while until all the adulation died down. It still hadn't stopped.

"The gallery shuts its doors at ten." He glanced over her satin smooth dark head. She wore her hair in a style he particularly liked if the woman could get away with it. A classic chignon that emphasized her enchanting swan neck. "I sincerely hope you're going to join us at dinner?"

She pressed her fingers to her temple.

"Please don't claim a headache," he begged, smiling into her eyes. "I promise you you're going to enjoy yourself. I've already met Ross, of course. I feel already he's just the right man to lead our expedition."

She allowed her eyes to appraise his height and his broad shoulders. A gentle giant but she had no doubt he could be incredibly tough when he had to be. "You don't strike me as the sort of man who needs anyone to lead him."

He gave her another charming smile. "As much as I hate to say it I'd definitely need an expert to guide me through Kakadu. This is your part of the world."

"Yet you've visited other extremely remote places. Very dangerous places as well."

"And I've counted on good people who know what they're about for survival."

She braced herself a little. He was very close, towering over her. So big, so solid, but marvellously nonthreatening. She had made a horrendous error in judgment with Blair but she knew in her bones this man would always deal with women gently. "I'm not exactly sure Ross has made up his mind, Mr. Langdon," she warned him.

"David, please."

"Isabelle." She spoke almost shyly, her creamy white skin colouring slightly. It was enormously appealing. Rumour had painted her a vain self centred creature who lived only for her own pleasure and conquest. He saw none of it. Perhaps tragedy had destroyed her confidence.

"It suits you," he remarked, his voice deep with more than a polite veneer. If he had to visualise Shakespeare's Dark Lady of the Sonnets, it would be Isabelle Hartmann. He surprised within himself not only fascination but a curious tenderness for this young woman with the purity and loveliness of a lily. She was wearing white to enhance the effect, one shouldered, a fluid column, no jewellery except for pendant earrings. Lustrous South Sea pearls appended from a diamond cluster. She wore no rings on her long fingered hands. No engagement ring. No wedding ring. Pearl painted nails. There again a puzzle. Would a woman so recently widowed remove clear evidence of her marriage? What did it say? She had gained no comfort there?

His topaz eyes glowed like a cat's without giving anything away, but Isabelle was aware he was noting every last little thing about her. Extraordinarily she welcomed it. One of the paradoxical facts of life. As big and masculine as he was, he didn't *threaten* her. Rather she felt in the presence of some powerful creature who for his own reasons had taken her under his protection. She had already noticed there was something distinctly leonine about him even to the tawny mane. She realised she too was taking stock, wondering how those thick waves would feel beneath her hands. To grasp them! To tug gently. It would be quite wonderful.

My God, she had to be mad!

"That's great! You two have finally met."

Each was so engrossed in the other they actually started when Samantha appeared at her brother's side, smiling her pleasure. She glanced at her watch excitedly. "Ten minutes to go then we can all get to know one another better. I have to admit I'm hungry. What about you, Isabelle?"

It was her moment to say she had a slight headache and would be returning to the hotel only someone as radiant and friendly as Samantha Langdon was hard to resist. David

Langdon said nothing, quietly waiting for her answer. She was forced to admit the fact he was going to be there had a huge bearing on her decision. She couldn't bring herself to ask why. Better that way.

"Perhaps a little," she smiled. "But I warn you. I'm not going to talk. I'm going to *listen*."

They all sat round a circular table, paired off as if it would have been obvious to an onlooker that Isabelle and Ross and David and Samantha were closely related. David's assistant Matt had a previous engagement to meet up with a friend staying at the Holiday Inn so the numbers were even. The restaurant was nowhere near as opulent as the restaurants Isabelle had frequented with Blair and their circle of friends. *His* friends really, part of the Establishment, grown up together, gone to the same schools and University, but the food was every bit as good. Over the last dreadful months it had been difficult just trying to swallow enough to stay alive but tonight sitting between David Langdon and her brother Isabelle found herself surprisingly hungry. Even the air around her had taken on a different quality. Maybe sanity wasn't staying away from people but joining them.

They all had different things for an entrée, though she and Jessica shared a range of appetisers, crudités and quails eggs and a beautiful Haloumi that came from Kangaroo Island and was much better than the imported. Samantha had sea scallops wrapped with bacon with a red wine sauce, David, pan fried prawns in potato waistcoats, Cyrus decided on abalone with shiitake and young salad leaves served in its beautiful ovoid shell and Ross stayed with one of his favourites, rice noodle cannelloni stuffed with the superb blue swimmer crab meat.

It was difficult not to mellow under the influence of such beautiful food and the excellent chilled chardonnay that accompanied it. Seafood figured heavily for the main course, magnificent lobster caught that very morning, coral trout off the Reef, and the superb eating fish barramundi for which the Top End was famous.

Ross glancing across at his sister found it deeply hearten-
ing to see her eating with apparent enjoyment, smiling fre-
quently at something David Langdon said to her, obviously at
ease with him. It was almost as if he had brought her to life.
There was colour in her cheeks. She looked very beautiful but
still dangerously vulnerable. Well, Langdon was a kind man.
He could see that. A gentleman. He was also very amusing, very
knowledgeable, and Ross had had ample evidence women
found Langdon extremely attractive. David Langdon had to be
one hell of a catch. It didn't occur to Ross that people said exactly the same thing about him.

Dessert was out of the way—the men had wanted it—the
women protested they had to mind their figures but Langdon
persuaded Isabelle to try a lime and ginger crème brulee. Coffee
after that, and the *real* discussion began.

Here it comes Samantha thought. He's going to make it perfectly plain he doesn't want me along. The Great White Hunter
on his men only expedition. Men she had to admit had a special camaraderie. In the space of a couple of hours she could
see her brother and Ross Sunderland had made a good connection. Something she could hardly say for herself and that com-
plicated man. It was easy to see both men would get along
indeed all three men had a lot in common, essentially men of
action living their lives outdoors for most of the time. Of course
women formed extraordinary bonds but in different ways and
usually it took longer. She and Jessica were long time close
friends but she could see she couldn't intrude on Isabelle's
space no matter how much she liked her. Isabelle had lost her
adored husband and she was wrapped in sadness. Nevertheless
it was lovely to see her responding to David's gentle masterly
hand. Her big brother was simply *the best*. There had been
women in his life of course, but apparently nothing so intense
it had made him want to enter into marriage. Marriage didn't
always culminate in happily ever after anyway. Before their parents had been divorced they'd become bitter enemies. Two bit-

ter enemies who had together created herself and David. When did a marriage go wrong? What happened to the spoken vows of love and commitment? In the end the only thing possible was for each to release the other. A sane person would stay away from marriage entirely.

She moved on to Ross Sunderland who knew all about parental marriage bonds broken and the grief that attended it. Certainly he was relaxing his guard. In fact he was showing himself to be excellent company but when his eyes fell on her she couldn't miss the challenging glint that sent tingles chasing down her spine. That in itself was unsettling. How could one be attracted to a man with an irresistible need to snap one's fingers at him at the same time?

Talk of Kakadu, the great national park brought the men alive. Twenty thousand square kilometres of crocodile infested rivers, low lying flood plains, rocky outcrops, waterfalls rain forest and woodlands dominated by the magnificent buttress of the Arnhem Land escarpment that ran for six hundred kilometres across the tropical Top End, one of the last great world wilderness areas. It had been established aboriginals had inhabited Kakadu for fifty thousand years. Neighbouring Arnhem Land was still inhabited by large numbers of Australia's indigenous people indeed Kakadu was under the custodianship of the traditional owners.

Ross and Cy were telling David about the world famous rock galleries of Nourlangie and Ubirr estimated at around twenty thousand years old and of great archaeological importance.

"Most of the paintings at Nourlangie are in the X-ray style," Ross said, leaning towards David like a man on a mission to sell the Top End. "Two phases descriptive and decorative. Extraordinarily these X-ray drawings depict the subject's internal anatomical features. Ibirr is another treasure house you'd need to see. You'll find the *Mimi* spirits depicted there. The aboriginals believe they live in the caves, even in the little cracks and crevices."

"To them, the *Mimi* are terrifying creatures," Cy eased in the comment.

Ross nodded. "Namargon, the Lightning Man is represented, stone axes growing from his head, arms and knees to strike the ground. He appeared when the region first experienced the great electrical storms of the Wet. The rock art is the region's major cultural heritage. It can't be missed."

"Take me there," David smiled. "I'm sold."

They got through almost another hour talking. David Langdon asked a great many questions. Cy and Ross answered them, taking turns, sometimes speaking together their enthusiasm was so great. Isabelle sat back quietly. Jessica smiled lovingly at her husband, Samantha inwardly was on tenterhooks. She couldn't bear to think for once she would lose out although Sunderland hadn't as yet agreed to act as their guide. His purpose on the whole seemed to be that of an arm chair guide, pointing out the very special areas of interests, the sacred sites, the extraordinary land forms and the spectacular escarpment country and the various hazards along the way which included the immensely dangerous giant saurians of the Alligator River, North and South, and the numerous billabongs and wetlands. Both he and Cy maintained if you treated the crocodiles with respect and didn't intrude foolishly on their territory no harm would come to you.

Samantha took that as a very good reason for being allowed to go along. It wasn't as though she was planning to come within patting distance of their hideous snouts. They weren't cuddly koalas, though even koalas being wild animals could inflict a lot of damage if they felt threatened.

David gave a satisfied sigh. "So are you going to be free to take us?"

For one dreadful moment it looked like Sunderland was about to say, no, only Samantha breathed a sigh of relief when his sister caught his eye and smiled. Isabelle knew he wanted to go. Ross loved being out in the wilderness. There were a few pressing commitments he would have to attend to before he went. Afterwards for the space of a few weeks of the trip he could delegate. Their overseer, Pete Lowell, was a good, dependable man. Their father had trained him.

"All right," Ross agreed, returning his sister's smile with some wryness. "I'll take you. That would be Matt, your assistant and yourself, I take it?"

Well you take it wrong, Samantha thought smartly, catching *her* brother's eye.

"I was hoping, Ross, Samantha could come," David said sounding thoroughly persuasive.

It was quite clear that didn't work on Sunderland. The animated expression on his lean handsome face changed abruptly. Samantha *willed* him to give in but he shook his head. "That would well and truly be bending the rules, Dave. It will be far from easy getting to the places you'd want to get your shots. I've seen your work. I know danger entices you. It's the same excitement as a safari only we don't get to kill magnificent wild animals as they did in the bad old days."

"What if we established camps?" David suggested, seeing Sunderland's point of view.

"And leave your sister on her own?" Sunderland's black brows shot up.

I'm not even Samantha, Sam thought. I'm "your sister."

David's topaz eyes moved to the silent Isabelle. "What if Isabelle came along? For all her lilylike appearance I expect she's a woman who could handle herself in the bush."

Yes, oh yes!

Samantha, mindful of what Isabelle had said to her, managed to hold her tongue but instead of shrinking away from the idea, Isabelle glanced down, her long lashes dark and heavy on her cheeks. She knew Ross had made it clear he didn't want Samantha on the trip which in all fairness she had to admit was in the wildest least explored area of the continent. On the other hand she could see Samantha had a positive yen for adventure.

She glanced up and caught David Langdon's golden eyes on her. Her pulses gave a mad little jitter as though he had actually touched her lightly. "Do I have to answer now?"

Her brother stirred restlessly. "Belle, would you really want to go along? You know as well as I do, it won't be any party. I think Samantha's initial enthusiasm for such a trip would be short lived. I can't keep my eye on her one hundred per cent of the time which means I can't guarantee her safety."

"Maybe David has the answer," Cy intervened mildly, thinking it was a bit of an awkward situation. "Make camp in a safe area. If there was any danger involved when David was taking his shots, the girls could stay together. That's if Isabelle consents to go."

"Come to think of it I'd like to go myself," Jessica gave her husband an arch look.

"No chance of your going without me," Cy grabbed her hand playfully.

"Doesn't that prove what I'm saying?" Ross asked. "Taking the women would slow us down too much."

"Come on, Ross!" Isabelle's eyes suddenly flashed giving a glimpse of the high spirited girl she had been. "You're telling me *I* couldn't keep up?"

Ross sighed. "You don't have the same level of fitness you used to have, Belle. In fact you look like a stiff breeze could blow you away."

Isabelle stared at him, outraged. "I do *not!*"

David Langdon broke in, holding up a large hand. "You honestly believe this trip could become too rough for the women, Ross?"

Ross nodded, giving Samantha a long speaking look. "I've already worked out the areas I'd want to take you. For that matter I'd bring along my own man. Cy knows him well and can vouch for him. His name is Joe Goolatta. He's a full blooded aboriginal elder, a fine man and a great bushman and tracker. He won't be a follower. He'll lead with me. This is *his* country. The crocodile is *his* totem. Believe it or not the crocs seem to recognise this. They sure don't with anyone else."

"Incredible!" David commented, having seen strange things himself in various primitive parts of the world. "The reason I wanted Sam to come along—apart from the fact I believed she would thoroughly enjoy it—is that Sam usually writes the text. She's very good at it."

"I agree." Ross nodded, moving an impatient shoulder. "Going on tonight's exhibition but couldn't she just as easily write the text from the finished product?"

"I'd be missing the *immediacy*." Samantha gave him an incensed glance. "I wouldn't be frightened if you left me alone back at camp. I'm not a wimp. Of course it would be wonderful if Isabelle could keep me company," she murmured, brushing back a silken slide of hair.

Only a fool let himself be manipulated by a woman. "Do you know how to shoot?" Sunderland asked her brusquely, watching that copper hair slide forward seductively again.

The challenge in her seemed to evaporate. "You mean a gun?"

"Certainly a gun," he clipped off. "A rifle. A .22?"

"No, sir!" Samantha glanced across at her brother for support. "I've never even seen a gun up close let alone handled one. I hate guns. They're horrible."

"And necessary if you're trying to protect yourself in the bush." Sunderland studied her as though she really belonged in kindergarten. "What do you do if a wild boar goes on the attack or a croc abruptly surfaces out of a pool and comes at you at speed. Aim a stone at it? What do you do when some member of the party inadvertently treads on a taipan? Throw a stick at it?"

Colour stained Samantha's cheek bones. "Would *you* mind not taking a chunk out me? I get your point, Mr. Sunderland." She really *loathed* this man.

"Well that's a first."

Watching the electric exchange Isabelle entered the fray. "But *I'm* good with a rifle," she said. It wasn't just women sticking together. What else? "Dad taught us both well."

Her brother looked like he thought the conversation had gone far enough. "Don't let your sense of derring-do get the better of you, Belle. Really think about it."

It was David who brought it to an end. "Perhaps that's the answer. Why don't we let you and Isabelle talk it over, Ross? I understand your concerns. I daresay in your position I wouldn't be prepared to take the risks either, but if Isabelle steps in, it sounds like we could reduce the risks considerably. Sleep on it. Maybe we can meet tomorrow in the morning seeing we're staying at the same hotel. Or did you want to get away early?"

"I ought to." Ross gave a slight frown. "But the morning will be fine. Belle can have a sleep in. I've agreed to be your guide, Dave, and that will stand. I know Samantha is angry at me but she doesn't actually know what she could be in for."

"Sleep on it, friend," David advised.

There were much fewer guests now. People had begun to leave. Cy stood up, holding his wife's chair. "On that note, we'll say good night. I have a feeling it will all turn out well. Jessica and I had best be off. We're staying with Robyn and her husband. They're sending a limo to pick us up, so I'd say it will be waiting out the front."

"We had a wonderful time," Jessica said, rising gracefully. "I loved your showing, David."

David also on his feet now, bowed slightly. "Great seeing you again, Jessica. And thanks for all your help." With one hand he held Isabelle's chair, catching her elusive, very beautiful perfume as she rose to her feet.

"Marvellous food!" Cy put in, sending David a friendly grin. "You can't do better than Ross for a guide," he added, throwing a glance at his friend who was starting to move back. "Isabelle's not bad either."

For a female Samantha started to say, then thought better of it. No point in angering Ross Sunderland until he'd made his decision. She took a precipitous step away from the table without looking, then realised with a pounding of the heart she'd all but bumped into him.

On a reflex his arm swiftly snaked around her waist holding her steady.

"Sorry!" she breathed, shocked by the sensation. "You're a very fast mover."

"I guess I am." His eyes locked into hers. He could feel the warmth of her body through the thin fabric of her dress. He soaked it up hungrily, tempted to spin her into his arms. He might have been fool enough to do it had they been on their own. And damn the consequences. He knew it by its name. *Temptation.* At least the others were momentarily distracted saying their goodbyes.

Samantha glanced back over her shoulder, her blood coursing at his closeness. Against his bronze skin his blue-green eyes were startling. His sculpted mouth wasn't all that far away. She only had to lean back further. She wondered what it would be like to have those clean cut lips pressed against hers. Deep and passionate. For he was a passionate man. She was sure of it.

"You can let me go now," she said tautly. His hand was singeing her flesh.

"Sure," he drawled, slowly withdrawing. "The last thing I want to do is unsettle you."

Male arrogance was in his very stance. "What makes you think you have?" she asked sharply.

He smiled, but didn't answer, malicious laughter in his sparkling eyes.

CHAPTER THREE

USED TO A predawn start Ross woke at the usual time even though he'd had what for him could only be described as a bad night. Mostly he was so dog tired after a hard day's work on the station he fell asleep the instant his head hit the pillow but here in this quiet air-conditioned hotel room his mind kept revolving around the problem of Samantha Langdon. And she was a problem. A *big* one.

Go away. Damn you!

Hell, it was almost a prayer.

Too late for that, Ross, old son. The inner voice answered. *She's got to you.*

That didn't mean he had to surrender.

He and Belle had talked well into the night, Belle arguing strongly for Samantha's inclusion on the trip. He told himself the thing that had clinched it was Belle's surprise desire to go. It was the first real interest she had shown in anything since she had come home after the loss of her husband. That in itself was encouraging but what, he wondered, had prompted the big upsurge of interest? It had to be something to do with the near instant connection she had made with David Langdon. Whatever it was it had energised her. He had seen with his own eyes the harmony that had flowed from one to the other. Langdon was a very motivated, very self-disciplined, powerful sort of man. He was also, as might be expected of an artist, a man of sensitivity, finely attuned to women. Belle liked him. Hell, he liked the man himself.

But Samantha?

He couldn't stop his body stirring. He could even *sense* her presence.

Why are you rejecting her, Ross?

He had tried to give Belle an answer but he knew she saw through him. The answer cut into the most primitive part of him. Part of his and Belle's unhappy past. Yet for all that he had finally agreed to take both Belle and Samantha Langdon along. The beginnings of a friendship was flowering between the two women. He couldn't say the same for himself and this copper haired woman. All bright things in nature could be dangerous. Dammit all he was *hurting*. He knew now he'd been hurting since he'd met her. That's what was making him so stubborn. Obdurate if you like. Up until now he'd negotiated easily enough through emotional entanglements—he'd had his share of girl-friends—but he simply couldn't do it with this woman. He'd hate to fall in love. *Really* fall in love. To want so much. To be left...*wanting*. Belle knew what a lot didn't. Underneath he was a pretty passionate guy. Passionate guys had to take care....

He braced his hands beneath his dark head going back over Cy's wedding. He'd had a little bit too much to drink. It was, after all, a very grand and happy occasion. Cy was over the moon, madly in love with his beautiful new bride, Jessica. He felt great for him. Cy was his pal. As best man he'd given a good speech and it had gone well. A mix of remembrances, mostly good, one or two touching, but on the whole leavened with humour. People had laughed even until tears came to their eyes.

The other three bridesmaids had accepted him completely as scion of a well respected family, Cy's best friend and some-one nice to know. Very pretty girls, all three, who'd enjoyed flirting with him. With his senses exquisitely sharpened he had flirted back when all he'd really wanted was his arms around *her.* The urge was so powerful and persistent that in the end he had surrendered to it. Besides, it was his *duty* to dance with the chief bridesmaid. It would have been a serious breach of etiquette not to.

She had looked like a man's dream come true. The smooth naked shoulders, the half naked back. The heart shaped dip of her strapless neckline revealed the creamy swell of her breasts and the shadowed cleavage. The material of her gown was something called *duchesse* satin. He understood that meant the fabric was thick, lustrous, supple. The colour, champagne with a blush of apricot, was perfect with her colouring. She didn't wear her hair free as she had done the first time he had seen her running down Mokhani's staircase. It was pulled back from her face, like the other bridesmaids and arranged in some full upturning roll at the back of her head, one beautiful silk flower to match her gown tucked behind her ear.

When he went to her, her face brightened. "Oh, Ross!"

"My dance, I believe." He put his arms around her, his need too great to be suppressed. She was heartbreakingly beautiful in her wedding finery, wearing Cy's gift to the bridesmaids, a drop pearl pendant on a fine gold chain around her long slender neck. Hers was an unusual gold with a single sparkling cognac diamond above it. Her earrings matched the colour, the pearls dropping from a series of tiny winking diamonds. He wondered if Cy had bought them as well or they were her own? What man wouldn't love to give her jewellery he thought. Cover her naked body with it.

"I really thought you didn't want to dance with me." Her expression was sweetly anxious as she looked up at him.

"Why wouldn't I want to dance with the most beautiful bridesmaid?" he had countered in that voice that was all wrong.

She'd smiled in a poignant way. "For one reason you've been having the most wonderful time with the others."

"That isn't the reason," he said.

Sparklelike tears rose to her eyes, heightening his desire for her that was growing beyond measure. Many eyes were following them. He was fully aware of that. She turned her head to acknowledge the smiles and nods from either side. "I'll remember this day forever," she said. "Jessica as radiant and beautiful as a bride should be. Cy so splendid and so much in love with her." She'd looked up at him. "I loved your speech too, Ross. It made us all laugh and cry."

"Is that why you've got tears in your eyes now?" He knew his grip had tightened on her. He could feel her trembling as though unprepared for what might ensue.

She blinked her damp lashes. "I didn't know I had."

"Well it's a time for high emotion after all." He was disgusted with the vaguely taunting way it had come out but unable to rein himself in. He wanted to cup her breasts; lean in to kiss her lovely mouth.

"Ross, what *is* it?" she had asked as though she could no longer cope with what was happening between them.

He hadn't answered. What could he say? *I want to take you to bed. Now!* Instead he began to dance her fast down the full length of the room, while the other guests laughed and clapped, standing back to give them a free path, thinking it all such glittering, good fun.

He remembered her lovely flush afterwards, her hand to her heart, and her carefully hidden agitation. She understood the strange ambivalence in him.

Blood was rushing through his entire body. He was conscious of his hard hurting erection. He couldn't continue to lie there thinking about her. He groaned and pushed up. He was tired of his own thoughts. Tired of being haunted by a woman with doe's eyes. Now he'd have to spend *weeks* with her.

Bronze brolgas struck a pose in an idyllic setting. In the luxuriant gardens that surrounded the hotel's swimming pool tropical plants abounded, gardenia, oleander, hibiscus, ginger, bougainvillea, beautiful orchids and bromeliads with their brilliantly coloured rosettes. Magnificent palms soared overhead shading an area that was perfect for swimming and light sunbathing. No one wanted to be exposed to the full force of the tropical sun even at this early hour. The turquoise pool looked wonderfully inviting, plenty big enough for a serious swimmer. Better yet, there was no one around. She would have it all to herself. She had plenty of time to do her usual laps before returning to her room to shower, shampoo her hair and get dressed.

Samantha dropped her hold-all on a teak recliner lavishly upholstered in broad bands of turquoise lime and aqua, then pulled her floaty caftan over her head. It matched her bikini, both in a vibrant botanical print. An expensive outfit considering the cover-up was see-through and didn't reach her knees and the bikini was so flimsy if it hadn't been guaranteed shrink proof she wouldn't have dared to expose it to water. Still if you had it you might as well flaunt it as her girlfriend, Em, always said at some point in their work-out at the gym. Samantha didn't take her slender figure for granted. She worked at keeping her body in excellent shape. The right food—not too much of it—except the occasional breakout, two nights a week at the gym, a run around the marina near her harbourside apartment every other day, surfing at the weekend at one of the beautiful beaches, Bondi, Tamarama, Bronte close by.

Oh that water looked good! She approached the deep end of the pool and dived in, not even surfacing until she had swum one hundred metres. There was a time at high school when the coach had tried to talk her into having a shot at the Australian Institute of Sport. She was good—she had even won a couple of Junior State titles—but she knew she didn't have the tremendous dedication that was needed to make it as an elite swimmer. Besides she had other goals. Mostly creative. It had come as a surprise to many of her friends when she had turned to writing and illustrating children's stories. They had thought she would try to make it into television but that wasn't her goal either. One day when she had enough maturity she would try her hand at adult fiction. One review of her last children's book suggested with her ability and "rich poetic voice" she would soon turn to something beyond her present scope.

Hopefully. That was all in the future.

She put a hand to her hair—she had woven it into a plait—ready to kick off again when she froze. Ross Sunderland was walking down the side of the pool dressed in shorts and an open casual shirt, with a towel over his shoulder. Just when she thought she would have the pool to herself! It was only a matter of time before he saw her. He was heading her way, his every movement filled with tantalising male grace. It was a daunting aura he exuded in her presence but she knew it was only a mask. She'd seen how sweet and gentle he was with his sister. David had really liked him—thought him remarkable—and her brother was a good judge of men.

Samantha kicked off again, determined not to allow him to upset her. She thought nothing of doing fifty laps, but not today. Her arms sliced through the water, while her legs scissored beneath the turquoise waters not making a splash.

Finally she had to stop at the shallow end to do something about her hair. It had come out of its plait, floating around her like a mermaid.

"How long are you going to keep it up?" he asked her.

She glanced up but the sun was in her eyes. Nevertheless she could see his wide shouldered outline. He had gone down on his haunches beside the edge of the pool.

"This is only a little paddle, okay?" She pressed her hair back with her two hands.

"You'd have fooled me," he mocked. "I thought you were going for Olympic gold."

"Don't worry, I could have made it." She indulged in a bit of wishful thinking.

"Amazing!"

"Well I won a couple of Junior State titles." She turned her head out of the direct line of the sun. Now their glances clashed. Brown velvet and blue-green ice.

"I bet in record time." Those shimmering eyes were moving over her face and the line of her shoulders just above the water.

"As a matter of fact, yes." She grasped the coping and pulled herself out, anxious to get her towel. As always his gaze made her giddy.

"Oh, Miss Langdon." He came to his impressive height, effectively blocking her way. "I'm sorry. Surely I haven't frightened you away?"

"No, I've got better things to do, that's all," she responded tartly. She had never been so conscious of her own body though he wasn't looking at her in any offensive way, rather with cool male appreciation. A connoisseur of women, which doubtless he was.

"Wouldn't it be an idea to race me?" he surprised her by suggesting.

"Good swimmer that I am—I'm sure you thought the best I could do was splutter and drown—I just *know* I wouldn't stand a chance," she replied.

"Why not give it a go just for the hell of it? You're very good. Very fast. I'm not nearly so efficient on the turns. Yours are quite professional."

"They ought to be. I spent enough time practising them." She moved her slim, shapely legs towards the recliner vowing there and then not to get into any competition.

"So is it a race or are you going to chicken out?" he called, feeling that edgy desire slice through him. It never went away. She had the most beautiful skin all over. The cream in the sun deepening to honey. Or as all over as he could see which happened to be a lot. "Who knows if you impress me I might just want to change my mind about the trip."

In the act of towelling herself down Samantha broke off. "I think you're hooked already." She might never be able to bring this man to his knees which she'd absolutely *love* but she knew enough to gauge he was powerfully attracted. It was something he also found unacceptable.

"What is that supposed to mean?" He came towards her so purposefully for a mad moment she thought he was going to pull her to him.

"Sad you're so aggressive." She had to make a real effort to steady her voice.

"I'm not usually." A faint smile touched the chiselled lips. "You've managed to tap into that vein."

"Why I wonder? Do I remind you of someone? A romance gone wrong?"

He measured her with those cool sparkling eyes. "Don't feel guilty on that account. I don't go in for failed relationships."

"But you are seeing someone aren't you?" she asked with growing provocation. "I couldn't help noticing the little brunette in the red dress last night. Not that she noticed *me*."

"Oh, she noticed you all right!" There was amusement in his expression. "But Julie is just a friend."

"Hoping for a whole lot more." Who could blame her for all she'd have to put up with?

"As is your Matt," he slotted in neatly.

That rattled her. "I though we'd settled that. Matt and I are not romantically involved."

"That's good, because I'd have grave misgivings about that."

"You're joking." She tossed back her hair. It was already drying in the heat.

"I'm not." He shrugged. "I don't believe in mixing business with pleasure." He half turned. "So are we going to race or not?"

Would it go better for her if she did? "On one condition."

He started to peel off his shirt, then the shorts, quite unselfconsciously, incredibly fit, incredibly lean. "I'm sorry, I'm not going to give you a start."

Damn if he didn't have the most marvellous body. She couldn't miss the perfectly honed musculature, the straight, strong legs. He was every inch a *man*. She had to swallow and glance away. "I don't think I need one. What I was going say was, if I win, you'll take me along on the trip?"

"And if you *lose?*" He looked at her with such intensity her heart leapt in her breast.

"I'll still be a good sport. And I'll still want to come."

His mouth compressed. "Oh, well, while we're at it, why don't you make a list of what you want me to do?"

"Well, you could be a little more, um, *friendly?*" she suggested sweetly.

"I might find that too exhausting. Are you ready?"

She slicked her hair back from her face. "I will be when you take your eyes off my legs."

Again he flashed that elusive white smile. "You can't wear a bikini like that and expect a man not to get excited. One hundred metres, two hundred, your call?"

Two hundred involved more turns. Valuable time could be lost at the turns even with top swimmers. "Two hundred," she said loftily, securing her plait with a band she fetched from her bag.

"Do you mind if we shake hands?"

"Of course not." Surprised she offered her hand, then saw his eyes. Eyes that sparkled and glittered with sardonic amusement.

She tried to withdraw her hand, only he caught her fingers with his own. A charge like dynamite rocked through her. She drew in her breath and jerked away. "Right, this has gone far enough."

"We were only holding hands."

"Yes, well…"

"Freestyle, I take it?" He helped her out.

"I can do the lot," she clipped off. "Freestyle, backstroke, butterfly, breaststroke. Take your pick."

"Why don't we stick to freestyle. That's *my* best stroke. On the count of three."

They hit the water together, sending up jets of spray. Samantha stayed underwater as long as she could before breaking into her stroke. Out of the side of her eye she could see him churning away, but she let him, keeping to her plan for a strong finish. It was *true*. She was better than him at the turns. At the one-fifty she was matching him stroke for stroke. They went down the pool together, slick as dolphins. She started to pick up speed, putting all her competitive spirit into it. Still she was racing an incredibly fit *man,* a good swimmer with a far superior reach. For an instant she thought he was dropping back, maybe letting her win. That made her angry. Then less than fifteen metres to go he shot past her like a torpedo, pulling his lean powerful body out of the water just as she touched the wall.

End of story.

He stretched out a hand. "Congratulations, Miss Langdon. I had to work hard to shake you. You're pretty good."

Her blood was pounding. Her heart was racing. She *had* to accept his hand. "That would have been my personal best," she admitted coming up out of the water in one graceful flowing movement.

"Truth is I used to swim for the team at University."

Her brown eyes flashed. "Dammit, don't you feel guilty not saying something about that at the beginning?"

"No." He smiled, the pool water still streaming over his darkly tanned, gleaming skin.

"You won because you're a *man*. A big man. I could have beaten a little guy," she pointed out.

"You could have beaten a guy *not* so little," he said wryly, wanting to pull her to him. Demand she forfeit a kiss.

"So are you going to let me come?" She looked appealingly into his eyes.

"You *lost,* remember?"

"Where's your sense of adventure?" Appeal turned to disgust. "I promise I'll keep a safe distance."

"Like now?" His eyes pinned her, held her in place.

"What do you mean?" She felt an instant's panic like some creature of the wilds caught in a high beam.

"Let's face it." His eyes moved lightly over her. "You've practically got no clothes on."

She shook her hair out of its plait. "Isn't that normal when one goes swimming?"

"Hey I'm not complaining." A smile touched his lips. "You're absolutely beautiful as I'm certain you've been told at least a thousand times. I'm only saying the kind of trip we're planning is no place to show off your sexual allure."

She recovered fast. "I'll be happy to wear dungarees," she said tartly.

"Not so great in the hot humid weather."

Samantha let out a long breath, preparing to move off. "I need to shower and wash the chlorine out of my hair before breakfast."

How he'd love to help her out!

And to think women had never been his problem! He watched her stalk off on those long golden legs, her colourful caftan doing nothing to hide the curves of her body. He began to ask himself yet again if he were mad.

Probably a bit.

While Ross and Samantha were trying to outdo each other in the pool David Langdon was renewing his acquaintance with the city of Darwin which he'd only visited in transit for some years. Long gone was the old Darwin of pioneering cattle kings, pearl trawlers, buffalo shooters, crocodile hunters and all kinds of adventurers, but the exotic *feel* to the place remained. Indeed it was difficult to compare the Territory's capital with any other city of Australia. It had the feel and smell of Asia. Asia was close enough, across the Timor and Arafura Seas. Darwin's full-on tropical climate and the city's rich racial mix—the Chinese remained the largest non-European population as well as the dominance of exotic Asian food made it unique. Loping teen-agers passed him, drinking milk from coconuts. A police car cruised by. The constable in the passenger seat waved casually. He waved back. He'd decided on making for the forty hectare Botanical Gardens. He knew it housed a range of tropical plants unequalled anywhere on earth. It certainly looked splendid, a luxuriant belt of green giving on to the turquoise waters of the huge harbour.

All around him were the signs of prosperity. The old isolated outpost, the centre for the gold rush of the 1870s, had grown enormously into a thriving capital. Tourism was now second only to the giant mining industry. The city had a very clean modern appearance due to the fact it had been rebuilt after Darwin had been destroyed in the 1974 Cyclone Tracy disaster. A new beginning had to be made virtually from scratch. Few buildings had survived consequently the present buildings had been built in contemporary style and designed to resist future cyclones. He sincerely hoped they would because another major cyclone would surely come again.

He realised he was impatient for their safari to begin. Champing at the bit really. He had photographed ancient ruins in the jungles of South East Asia, the beautiful stone temples of Angkor Wat and elsewhere, Thai kings palaces, the wonderful temple ruins of Borobudur in Indonesia, built by the Buddhist rulers the Sailendras in the 700s. He had photographed the great hardwood forests of Borneo and Java, teak and ebony, but he had never ventured into his own country's greatest wilderness area, Kakadu, the jewel in the Top-End crown and the giant among Australia's great national parks. The park was jointly controlled by the traditional Aboriginal owners and Parks, Australia. He also knew controversy had long raged between the conservationists and those wishing to exploit the incredibly rich reserves of uranium and other valuable minerals in the area. Ranger Uranium Mine and Jabiru, one of four major mining settlements in the Territory lay within the boundaries of World Heritage listed Kakadu. He'd like to gain access to both Jabiru and Ranger. He was relying on Sunderland to get permission from the mines' management. He knew they had to go through the traditional owners to visit certain parts of Kakadu and its sacred sites. No doubt about it. He felt *inspired*.

To some extent he knew the expanding euphoria had to do with meeting a certain woman. He had allowed himself to yield to it. Yet she was a mystery woman who had become the subject of cruel gossip. A sexually exciting woman who could play on a man's deepest emotions. Sympathy for her came all too easily for him but he had to concede he had no real knowledge of her to rely on.

Jump in and you might find the water's too deep.

He was about to cross the broad esplanade that ran parallel to Bicentennial Park when he saw another group of teenagers, with spiked black hair—dressed in T-shirts and colourful board shorts—cutting off the progress of a young woman he recognised even from a distance as Isabelle. She would be impossible to miss in a crowd.

Immediately his protective instinct went into overdrive. This wasn't just any woman although he would have made it his business to see what was going on. This was a woman he had related to on the deepest level. A kind of primal thing.

And don't you forget it!

Were they teasing her, annoying her, threatening her. What? She was a beautiful young woman on her own. There weren't all that many people about at that hour and it was the weekend. Stern faced he made short work of closing the distance between them while the youngsters broke off what they were saying to stare back at him in perturbation judging from their expressions.

What they saw was a *big* man, with powerful shoulders, his movements expansive and totally balanced. His tawny hair glowed in the sun. Clearly this was a man not to be trifled with. For that matter he looked like a lion full of pride coming to the defence of its mate.

"Anything the matter, Isabelle?" He stopped beside her, towering over the group as he checked her expression.

She looked up at him. Exposed to his mellow, charming side she now saw the combative daunting male. Well it was a long time since a man had had such concern for her, outside her own brother. "Nothing, David," she answered quickly, seeing how it might have looked to him. "These young people are my friends. I've known them since they were children. Say hello to Mr. Langdon, kids. He's a famous photographer. This is Manny and Jimmy and Charlie Chun Wing." As she spoke she laid a gentle hand on each boy's shoulder.

"Hello there. It makes us very happy to meet you." The eldest, Manny, the spokesman gave a big toothy smile, while the others executed modified bows that looked quite natural.

"I'm so sorry if I startled you," he apologised, his expression lightening. "I rather jumped to the wrong conclusion. I should have realised, Isabelle, you would know a great many people in Darwin."

"You thought we were annoying her?" Manny asked as if that were the last thing in the world they would do.

"How wrong I was, Manny. I can see none of you would do such a thing."

"Never!" Manny shook his jet black head gelled into upstanding spikes. "Nobody could be as good to us as the Sunderlands. Miss Isabelle's father set up Mum and Dad in our shop. My grandma and my Aunt Sooky used to work at the house. That's where Nan met my Grandpa. On North Star."

"So you see, David, we go a long way back," Isabelle glanced up at him with a little smile. "Please tell your parents I'll call on them soon, Manny."

"I know they would *love* to see you," Manny who was maybe sixteen responded with great dignity.

"Nice kids," David murmured, after the youngsters had gone on their way with much waving.

"Yes, they are. Manny's very clever. He plans to be a doctor."

"Marvellous, a success story," he said gently.

"I hope he makes it." She started to walk with him, recovering her head and shading her face with the wide brimmed straw hat she had dangled in her hand. They moved together through the entrance gates of the park, the dark green background of magnificent tropical trees animated by shafts of golden sunlight. Beautiful and welcoming as the Gardens were they also performed the practical task of providing a huge area of shade and protecting the city from much of the buffeting winds and torrential rains during the Wet.

Isabelle breathed in the air that wafted from the gorgeously perfumed shrubs in bloom. It was as powerful as any aphrodisiac. "There was a time when Manny's family was desperately poor. Cyclone Tracy wiped out their farm. Their uncle Frankie was killed, poor man. They were such hard workers Dad thought they deserved a helping hand, so he bought them a shop. Fruit and vegetables. They're experts at growing and selling."

"And the conditions would be much like Southern China," he commented. "Your father must have been a generous and kindly man."

Tears stung her eyes. "His good deeds were legendary. Ross is carrying on the tradition."

"You and your brother are very close." Though he dipped his head, he couldn't see her clearly. Enchanting as that daisy decked hat was, the wide brim did a good job of shielded her beautiful face from his view.

She let him have a glimpse of her aquamarine eyes. She was slightly flushed and not he thought from the mounting heat of the day. "You're bound to find out sooner or later, if you don't know already, David." Her tone implied he did. "Our mother left us when we were children. Neither of us thought it possible our parents would ever split up. They seemed so happy. We were *all* happy. A united family. Dad worshipped her."

"What happened?" he asked quietly.

She bit her lip and shrugged. "I suppose it was all meant to be. But after that I was never quite sure how my own life was going to turn out. Badly as it happens. My mother was visiting another branch of the family in England and fell in love with a distant cousin. It must have been something quite overwhelming. Something that robbed her of all control. My mother was not the frivolous type. Far from it. I remember her once saying nothing was better than a stable marriage. My God!"

"There's a lot of pain in passion, Isabelle."

She looked away at a great circular flower bed flaming with colour. "You don't have to tell *me!*"

So she had been madly in love with her husband.

"But, we have choices in life, David. There must be a moment when we can pull back. My mother didn't. She gave in to the feelings she had for this man. He ruined any hope she would come back to Dad although she wanted custody of us. Or at the very least me, the girl. Ross was the heir. Males are always on the inside track, especially when it comes to running the family business."

"You felt some resentment about that?"

She shook her head. "No, not at all. Just a simple statement of fact. The fact is I couldn't run North Star. You have no idea what's involved. One really does need a *man,* a strong man to handle most of the problems. Ross was reared to succeed Dad. No one could have stepped into the role better. Actually Ross feels even more strongly than I do about our mother's defection. No way would he have gone to her. How wildly unfair that would have been to our father. We were tied to him through love and blood and pride in our pioneering family and the land. A judge from the family court talked to us privately. We told him we would never leave our father. We loved him and wanted to stay with him. We didn't in fact want to see our mother."

Her voice was expressionless, hiding he felt sure a torrent of emotions she had locked away.

"I understand your feelings at that time, Isabelle, but do you *never* miss your mother?" After all he and Sam knew a whole lot about hurt.

She lifted her head, her expression brooding. "If I were honest, I'd tell you I've missed her every day of my life, but that doesn't change the fact I regard her as a traitor. I believe treason is punishable by death."

"You wanted her dead?"

She turned her slender back to him but he could see her shoulders trembling.

"I'm sorry, Isabelle." He had to ball his hands into fists lest he place them on her shoulders...those smooth fine boned shoulders.

"Of course not." She turned back, but her eyes were very bright. "Just a figure of speech. I'm really rather a damaged person, David."

He considered her gravely. "Aren't you being a bit hard on yourself?"

"No harder than the gossip." She laughed, but the flowering colour left her cheeks.

It wasn't possible not to reply. "You mean that things weren't well between you and your husband?"

She nodded. "You got it in one. The best way, I suppose, is to ignore it. I suspected you might have my history at your fingertips."

"Why would you think that?" he asked and waited.

"People talk wherever they are. Sydney, Darwin. Nothing too obvious last night, not with Ross around, but enough to cloud people's once good opinion of me."

"So what are you going to do about it? Put them straight?" He stared into her beautiful, black fringed, eyes.

"David, I don't much care. I am what I am. I've never tried to present myself as something different. Anyway, I was talking about my mother. You're too good a listener. For years she wanted me to come to England for the holidays—Dad wouldn't have stopped me—he loved me too much, but I refused to go. For Ross and for me—more so for our father—it was a grief so deep nothing, not even time, could heal the scars."

"So you learned to live without her?"

They walked on, keeping to the golden-green shade. "It

wasn't easy but I had a wonderful father and a wonderful brother."

"And a wonderful husband?" He realised he shouldn't have asked her but he couldn't stop himself.

That was his *public* image anyway. "I can't talk about him, David." At least that was the truth.

"Forgive me. That's understandable. It's been such a short time. I've no wish to upset you."

She could admit one thing however. "I rushed into marriage," she said. "Maybe it was the loneliness we Outback women endure. So much of Dad's and Ross's time was taken up with station affairs. I did my bit. I ran the domestic side and I handled a lot of office work, but I was on my own for much of the time."

"You could have left?"

Her beautiful eyes slanted up at him. "Of course I could but I wasn't fully *free*. My love for my family made up for a lot. I would have gotten around to it, if it hadn't been for Dad. He was bereft without the woman he'd made his life. I like to think I gave him emotional support even when he told me straight out I wasn't to sacrifice my life for him."

So she was far from selfish. She had a heart. "How did you meet your husband?"

"Why d'you ask?"

He captured her in profile. "I confess I want to know." In fact it seemed to matter greatly.

She took a long moment before she answered. "I was visiting a friend in Sydney. Her family was always on the social circuit. I'd only arrived that very day. Tanya was going to some big party hosted by Blair's mother at their palatial harbourside home. Blair's stockbroker father died of a massive heart attack a few years before. Tanya asked if I could come and Evelyn Hartmann said yes. It was there I met Blair. A fairy tale beginning without the fairy tale ending. Of course I failed to notice that Evelyn didn't like me from the start, but Blair fell in love with me. I was dumbfounded how quickly."

"So for you it wasn't love at first sight?" he asked after a bit, somewhat shamed by the feeling he was glad that wasn't so.

"I'm afraid I missed that experience, David." It wasn't a completely honest answer given her extraordinary reaction to *him*. For that she felt guilty as though she had broken a serious rule, almost a taboo. So recently widowed in the worst of circumstances, she had no *right* to be drawn to another man.

"Do you have someone you…care about?" He could be living with someone for all she knew.

"No." He answered simply. "I have quite a lot of women friends. I like women. I enjoy their company but to be honest I've spent much of my time travelling the world, particularly South East Asia. I studied architecture as you probably read last night. I have an architectural degree but I only practised for a couple of years before I moved on. I wanted to see the world and I did. In the course of seeing the world I found my first love. Photography. I've been lucky. I'm able to do something I love and get very well paid for it."

"You've been to the war zones as well."

He nodded, terrible memories suddenly crowding in on him. "The horror you've heard about and see on the television isn't exaggerated. The reality is far worse. I had to pull out of it for a while. The sheer scale of the human suffering became unbearable and I came to realise I was highly likely to get killed which wasn't going to help anyone. This breathing space is in the nature of therapy. It's impossible not to witness humanitarian disasters without coming away unscathed."

"I would think so," she said quietly. "The television coverage is disturbing enough."

He sighed deeply. "We're truly blessed living in Australia. From all I've seen it's something to celebrate." He paused and looked around him, deciding to change the subject. "It's remarkable to see how Darwin, not so long ago a frontier town, is booming."

"Yes, it's made a huge leap," she said, a proud Territorian.

"Strategically it's become very important. Our Defence Forces are stationed here. The victims of the Bali bombing too were flown straight to Darwin Hospital. I'm sure the close proximity and the skill and dedication of Darwin's doctors and nurses saved lives."

"Absolutely," he agreed. "That rocked us, Bali, so close to home. The shock waves haven't gone away any more than 9/11. It's a deeply troubled world."

"On top of all that the tsunami."

"Yes indeed." His strongly hewn features tightened. "My heart bleeds for the people and the places I came to know and love. I spent a lot of time in Thailand and Indonesia. I've holidayed in Phuket many many times, journeyed through Indonesia, visited the Maldives like so many other Australians. I could have even been there. The wrong place at the wrong time." He released a sigh, glanced at his wristwatch. "I suppose we should go back."

"Good heavens, is that the time?" She glanced at her own watch in amazement. Time had flown. "I've enjoyed our walk. And our talk."

"So have I," he said lightly. No way could he allow himself to show his private feelings. "Has Ross made up his mind do you know?"

"To take Samantha?"

"She'll be bitterly disappointed if she can't go along," David said. "Sam can handle herself, but of course I don't want to go against Ross's wishes. I appreciate we're on the verge of the Wet. It would be a matter of getting in and getting out."

"And quickly, taking our signals from the land and the sky. Joe Goolatta will be invaluable there. He's positively uncanny, but this is his land. Filming in far North Queensland you must know what it's like on the verge of the Wet."

"Of course. Some years back I took a helicopter flight from the bauxite town of Weipa in the Gulf to a mineral survey camp near Cape York. It was absolutely extraordinary. One of the great trips of my life. To see that prodigal wilderness from the air was fascinating. Great sluggish rivers twisting back on themselves like the Great Rainbow Snake of aboriginal legend. Hundreds and thousands of birds in the swamps many miles long. The Top End of the continent is still a no-man's land to most of us. Remote, barely accessible, certainly not in the Wet."

She nodded. "It's a pity, tourists, unlike the locals, never see this part of the world at its most spectacular when the wilderness bursts into fruit and flower. The billabongs and lagoons swell to overflowing with the rushing flood waters. Trickling waterfalls turn into mighty torrents. The wetlands abound with birds and I have to say crocodiles. The plains turn a lush green. It's Nature at its most powerful. But the tourists are back home by December before the deluge begins. It's all about picking exactly the right time. Which is what you're trying to do. We've already had a few spectacular lightning storms which will increase. But obviously around now is when you're going to get your most dramatic results. We've come to believe as the aboriginals do the Wet and the Dry is an oversimplification. The aborigines recognise at least six seasons, maybe seven signified by the flowering and fruiting patterns of food plants and the migratory and breeding patterns of birds and other animals. They are so attuned to the land they understand it as few white people do." She lifted her head to ask, "You use a digital camera?"

"Just about everything is digital these days, but a lot of the time I prefer to use film. A large format panorama. I've agreed to let Matt, my assistant, take some shots for part of the book so he'll be coming along all going to plan. I'd like to help him out. He's a good photographer but he needs to develop his 'eye.' Sam will do the text. Now she really does have an eye. Her children's books—they require a flight of imagination—are marvellously entertaining and her illustrations quite magical. She's very talented is my little sister. One day I believe she'll make a name for herself."

"She's already started." Isabelle smiled. "All right, David, I'll put you out of your misery. Ross and I counted up all the risks and at the end of it I managed to convince him it might be a very good idea to take two women along. In fact I'll make it my business to see Samantha has the loveliest time. It will do me good too to get out of the house. I've done so much brooding I sometimes feel I'm going mad. This is Gunumeleng by the way. The trip couldn't be contemplated if we wait much longer for Gudjeuk when the Wet is really unleashed. It won't be anything out of the ordinary if a cyclone or two blows in. But nothing on the horizon so far." She lifted her head, seeking his expression. "So does that make you happy?"

"That you're coming?"

The way he said it, the look in his topaz eyes made her catch her breath. Telltale colour spread along her cheekbones. "That *Samantha is.*"

Smiling, he took her elbow as they crossed the broad street. "Isabelle, I'm happy on *both* counts."

CHAPTER FOUR

THINGS moved very quickly after that. By midafternoon Monday they were all assembled on North Star ready to make their journey into Kakadu the next morning. They were to approach the great national park from its western side.

The land baked under a peacock blue sky but each afternoon there had been an ominous build up of cloud heralding spectacular electrical storms with lightning so bright it wounded the naked eye. Their trip had to be fitted in to the brief period before the rains came in earnest and the plains were inundated.

That night they dined in rural splendour in the homestead's formal dining room which these days Isabelle told Samantha as they prepared the evening meal together was rarely used. She and Ross always ate in the breakfast room off the enormous kitchen. No wonder! Samantha thought. The size of the homestead and its interior spaces obviously reflected the pioneering cattle man's idea of his castle in the wilds where wide open spaces were both expected and respected. The dining room was *huge*. Ideal for anyone planning a wedding banquet. As it was they sat at one end of the mahogany table which Samantha had set using beautiful buttercup yellow line and lace place mats with matching napkins. Isabelle had let her choose from a dizzying array of table linen bought over the years, loads of it never taken out of its cellophane packaging. Samantha had been in and out of many beautiful houses back home in Sydney but none so steeped in the pioneering tradition. She could settle down here she thought quite seriously. Love of Nature and this was Nature on the grand scale was an important part of her.

On arrival she had found the white-washed homestead built of stout timbers enormously picturesque. She could see herself sketching it in her mind's eyes, little aboriginal spirit imps with big liquid black eyes peeking out of all the trees in the luminous green jungle that surrounded the house and protected it from the winds. Buttresses of monster shade trees supported staghorns and elkhorns the likes of which she had never seen. Beautiful orchids thrived out in the open or burst out of the trees. Vivid vandas and dendrobiums, cymbidiums with spikes six feet long and the showiest of orchids the cattleyas in myriad varieties. Terrestrial orchids too popped out of fallen tree trunks or the fallen bark that was piled up beneath the trees. Her eyes were dazzled by the blazing bougainvillea; the familiar purple cascading from every trellis and fence but closer to the house there were other colours, the modern hybrids, white, pink, orange, bronze, crimson and violet. The vibrancy of the colours set the timber house a-shimmer.

Mangoes, their cheeks blushed with colour, the size of small pumpkins, were scattered beneath the trees. Dozens had rolled out onto the pathways that crisscrossed the home gardens. It was, she was told, a bumper year.

Standing on the gravelled drive way staring up at the homestead she was roused to say: "This is *amazing*, Ross. It's like some exotic film set."

"Glad you like it." He was hurting not to lean down and kiss her. She looked radiant in the humid heat, her long copper hair pulled back from her face in a pony tail. Her lovely, touchable skin was flushed with colour. Her eyes glowed, her expression dazzled, maybe overcome. He liked that. Her reaction to his home.

For the homestead was lovely. Two storied, set in some ten acres of gardens that formed the main compound. Basically a rectangle, deep verandahs extended across the front of the house on both levels, running down the sides of the house. Mahogany shutters protected high arched doors that marched in pairs down the lengthy expanses of the verandahs. Inside the high and handsome ornately carved double doors the entrance hall was revealed to Samantha's fascinated eyes.

"Wow! This is bigger than my apartment. What would it be like to actually live here?"

"I don't know. I've never lived anywhere else. You have an apartment?" He gave her his sardonic glance.

"Did you think I lived in a back alley?"

"You could live at home with mother," he suggested mildly, nodding at Isabelle who was showing David and Matt into the house.

She took a deep breath. "Mother has never asked me to move in with her. She has remarried. I don't like her husband." In fact she loathed her mother's second husband—she never would say her *stepfather*. He was an enthusiastic toucher so much so that when they met up she torpedoed past him so he couldn't grab a hold.

"Hard to describe love isn't it?" Ross mused, momentarily lost in his own thoughts. "What *is* it?"

"What you feel for your sister and I feel for my brother," she suggested.

"I'm talking about romantic love."

"An utterly crazy longing. Mostly for the wrong person."

"At least on that we agree," he said crisply. "So when was the last time you had this utterly crazy longing?" He stood watching as she moved gracefully around the hall, placing a gentle finger to the large Cambodian tapestry that hung on one wall.

"The last time?" She considered. "That's easy. To beat you in the pool." There was a circular library table holding a large eye catching arrangement of a giant tropical leaves, palm and monstera, setting off the living fire of the exotic bird of paradise, with sprays of ginger and heleconia, Samantha guessed must have come from the garden. It was easy to comment on it, thus changing the subject. Beyond a wide arch was the staircase with a tall lead light window above the first landing. Multicoloured rays poured through it. She moved to get a better look at this work of art, her own head on fire as the sun's beams fell directly on her.

What was depicted was a lagoon of water lilies, edged by reeds. Glorious blues and greens and amethysts were used, with the contrast of rose pink and liquid silver for the glinting water. It was a jewelled canvas of glass.

"Art Nouveau?" She turned to ask him then drew in her breath sharply. He was a lot closer than she thought.

"You're more in touch with all that than I am," he shrugged, too busy admiring the effect of the sunlight on her glorious hair. He found himself thinking at least one of her children, if she had them, would inherit that copper hair. "Right period. It's the work of a Japanese artist who happened to be a pearl diver on the side."

"Art Nouveau borrowed Japanese stylish features," she commented. "It's very beautiful. How do you protect it during cyclones and torrential storms?"

"It's boarded up. The shutters, obviously, are on the outside. Want me to show you to your room? It's already been prepared for you by Mrs. Lowell. That's our overseer's wife. She keeps an eye on the house when we're away. We used to have a permanent housekeeper but she left after my father was killed. It was all too much of a shock for her."

"I imagine it would have been," she said gently, the weight of his own grief coming at her.

Samantha preceded him up the stairs hearing her brother's deep cultured voice from somewhere at the rear of the ground floor. She gave into a simple impulse and waltzed into her allotted bedroom, not quite sure if she wasn't in the middle of a dream.

"Oh this is lovely. Thank you." She looked around her with evident delight.

"It's not mandatory to like everything, Samantha." He stood

in characteristic pose, handsome head thrown up, one hand speared into the pocket of his jeans. She had a way to her all of her own. As if a ring of light surrounded her.

"I can't help it," she exclaimed, going to try out the springs of the bed, like a child, checking its bounce. The bed was hung with billowing pale yellow mosquito netting that matched in colour the drapes at the arched doors. A big ceiling fan shaped like a flower whirred overhead, cooling·the air and ruffling the filmy curtains. An antique cabinet faced her, an elaborately carved chest at the end of the bed, carved chairs with aqua cushions. She spread her hands on the duvet, a cool shade of lime-green covered with tropical blossom. The bed skirt was aqua. A life-size ceramic brolga stood in one corner, an Asia folding screen in another.

"This is absolutely beautiful!" she said. "The pity of it is I'm only here for *one* night."

Which ought to have pleased him, but it didn't. But then she had many spells at her disposal to cast. "Well make the most of it," he said crisply, discovering the sight of her poised so gracefully on the bed, slender arms to either side of her was unsettling him. "You could be spending quite a few in pouring rain."

She stood up as though she divined his odd mood. "You're not a bit of fun are you?"

"Whereas you're hell bent on being an adventuress. No, I'm the serious type," he mocked her, supporting his long lithe body with one arm propped against the solid antique cabinet.

"Then I'm sorry I'm annoying you with my girlish chatter." She looked about her. "Is it all right if I explore? This is all so glamorous!"

"Sure!" He gave a shrug, then surprised himself by saying, "I have to make a last minute check around the station in about a half an hour. You can come if you like."

Her expressive face lit up. "Hallelujah! So there *is* a nice part of you?"

"The bumpy part will come later." He crossed to the door,

turning to flick a searing glance over her. "Don't wear the shorts."

She gave voice to mild exasperation. "What is it with you and my clothes?"

"I apply common sense. What else? There isn't a plethora of gorgeous looking leggy females around here. I don't want my men getting all steamed up."

"Bless you!" She looked back with bright challenge. "It's not like I could do the same for *you?*"

He narrowed his eyes. "My dear Miss Langdon, I run from trouble. I'm dedicated to North Star."

"Until you sort yourself out?"

"I beg your pardon?" He drilled her with a long stare.

"Sometimes I speak without thinking."

"So I've noticed." He proceeded on his way, throwing over his shoulder. "I'll have your things sent up. Meet me in the hall in around twenty minutes."

"Right, boss," she answered smartly.

"Don't push it."

"I wouldn't do that. Not to *you.*" *You arrogant so and so.*

"It seems to me you like living life on the edge." He turned to face her. "Another thing."

"I'm all ears." She pantomimed the act.

"Leave Matt alone."

She took that as censure. "Come again?"

"You heard the first time."

"You mean I'm not to speak to Matt at all? He's my friend. You've got to be joking."

"I don't know whether you've noticed, but I'm not one for jokes. I just don't want to bump into you locked in his arms."

She could feel the colour flood her cheeks. "Funny I can think of worse things like—"

"Don't say it." He shook his head warningly. "You can talk all you like. Just remember to put off all thoughts of romance until the end of the trip."

Her face, always an animated mirror of her emotions betrayed temper. "You must be one of the biggest wowsers on the planet."

"Well of course I am!" He laughed, his blue-green eyes asparkle.

The whole effect couldn't have been more sexy, but Samantha determinedly ignored it.

"The fact you're not all that interested in Matt doesn't mean he isn't anxious to make it with you. Forewarned is forearmed as my dad used to say."

"I've got another one for you," she answered tartly. "All work and no play makes Ross a dull boy. But thank you anyway. I promise I'll take to heart everything you've said."

But she wasn't counting on what life on safari might offer.

They were well underway by midmorning of the following day. Samantha had never been so close to Nature. This magnificent wilderness had to be one of the most beautiful places on earth. It was a wild paradise simply teeming with life. She rode in the lead 4WD with the Boss Man as she had taken to calling Ross Sunderland to herself. He certainly looked the part in khaki bush shirt and hard wearing khaki trousers, a tan leather belt slung around his waist, a cream Akubra with a crocodile skin band on his dark head.

A commanding presence.

And don't you forget it!

She could scarcely walk by him without wanting to drop a mock curtsy, except he might take it as his due. Joe Goolatta, one of the most engaging characters she had ever met, rode in the back, the two men keeping up non-stop commentaries solely for her benefit. Between the two of them it was all marvellously entertaining and educational as it was meant to be. It both surprised and pleased her enormously to see how fond of the old aboriginal the hardhearted Boss Man was. He made no bones about it. It was equally clear Joe Goolatta worshipped

Ross Sunderland without being in any way subservient. The two men fenced lightly, Goolatta teasing from time to time, which incredibly Boss Man took. Joe had known Sunderland since he was a child and it showed in his relaxed affectionate attitude. She began to think about what Sunderland would have looked like as a little boy. Not a shy nervous kid that's for sure. A haughty little prince.

She found herself laughing a lot listening with aesthetic pleasure to the cadences of the men's voices. The Boss Man's clipped, dark timbred, educated, the older man's basso deep and wonderfully melodious.

As they drove deeper into the great national park Samantha looked all around her with a sense of buoyancy and privilege. Some kilometres back they had passed a Top End safari taking a break.

"Only for the young and fit," Ross commented. "No more than nine a trip. Back packers love it. Young people looking for adventure. Those safaris are no sight seeing tours. It's a learning experience and as I said they have to be young, fit and strong. They have excellent guides."

"So what do they do? What do they see?" Samantha asked.

"Much of what we're going to do," he shrugged, "only we'll explore further a field. Go where no man has ever gone before, in Star Trek speak. That lot back there are on their way out of the park. I'd say it was one of the five day tours. Camping out under the stars, bar-b-ques around the camp fire, long bush treks, cooling off at any number of the park's falls. No crocs. There are some seventeen permanent water falls even in the Dry. Jim Jim plunges two hundred metres in a single drop. They'd have seen the estuarine crocs from a boat as we will. We have a boat on standby. That's all been arranged. For certain they would have taken in the beautiful ancient aboriginal rock art at Nourlangie and Uburr. Much of it is well in excess of twenty thousand years old, priceless to man for its spiritual and cultural significance. Joe can tell you all about the

Dreamtime and Mythology of the sites. Joe is a tribal elder. The origin of Kakadu in case you don't know is a breakdown of *Gagudju* the name of the aboriginal tribe who lived in the area for more than fifty thousand years."

"It beggars the imagination." Samantha turned her head to smile at the aboriginal elder. "I'm so looking forward to seeing these magical sites with my own eyes, and with such authoritative guides. This is a marvellous experience for me. I'm picking up so much inspiration from *everywhere!*" She waved a hand. "I write children's books, Joe."

"So Ross told me," Joe answered in his deep tones.

"Do you want to see what I can do?"

"Sure." He laughed warmly, having taken to this beautiful, friendly creature who appeared to have no pretensions at all. A far far cry from Miss Isabelle's cruel mother-in-law.

With no more ado, Samantha reached into the hold all at her feet, extracted a sketch pad and a charcoal pencil and went to work.

"No looking," she warned Sunderland.

"Right!" He gave an amused grunt. He made a brief check in his rear vision to see their back up vehicle driven by David. It was holding to their speed, a short distance behind. So far the trail was broad and easy to follow but it wouldn't be long before the countryside became rugged with grasses growing ten feet tall. The black soil plains were relatively park like with large stands of pandanus, vast grassy expanses and sculptured stone outliers that had been separated by time and erosion from the mighty Arnhem Land escarpment.

A few minutes later, Samantha tore off a page and passed it back to Joe who took it in his weathered hand.

His grin faded. "My, my, Miss Sam. You've done what no other person has even done. You've drawn me."

"Like it?"

He broke into a sardonic chuckle. "I don't look as good as this."

"Show me." Sunderland put up his left hand to take the drawing.

"I could have done better," Samantha said quickly. "The track is a bit bumpy."

Sunderland held the wheel and cast his eyes down. "You don't need excuses."

"What *do* I need?" She fixed her eyes on his strong handsome profile.

"Why ask? Congratulations, of course." He threw her his rare devastating smile. "This is Joe to a T."

Samantha blushed at the sincerity of his tone. "Why thank you," she said jauntily. "Do you want one of you?"

He turned his dark head. "Don't you want to wait until you know me better?"

There was that glitter in his eyes that thoroughly unsettled her, but she managed to keep her voice even. "Okay, I'll wait. You can give that back to Joe now."

"I reckon you should have that framed, Joe," Sunderland laughed, passing the sketch back over his shoulder.

"I will," Joe replied, quite seriously. "You're an artist, Miss Sam," he offered homage.

"I'm getting there," Samantha answered modestly. "Would it be *suitable* do you think, Joe, for me to try to interpret aboriginals legends in my stories. I would never want to offend your people."

"Can't see how you'd do that, Miss Sam," Joe replied after a minute or two's consideration. "I think you're a very sensitive young lady who might well be able to see and understand our magic. I have many many myths and legends I can tell you. So much is being lost. Maybe you can save a little bit of my culture."

"That's a very great compliment, Miss Langdon," Ross said, intrigued by the whole thing. Miss Samantha Langdon was far from being just a pretty face, she fell into the multi-talented category.

"And I'm duly mindful of it." Samantha returned his sidelong glance, accepting the fact this man thrilled her to her core.

Did he know it? She hoped not. She had to be very, very careful he wouldn't latch on. But oh, he left her shaken. Just being beside him produced a degree of sexual arousement hardly imaginable with anyone else. Nothing much she could do about it either. Her body was releasing a whole host of biochemicals causing this tremendous rush of sensations she rationalised. It mightn't have been love at first sight given the curious sexual hostility both had experienced when they'd first met—but it was something momentous. She'd had her share of boyfriends, some good, some not so good, but never had she felt this *intense* attraction. Even intense didn't come close. Knee buckling was better.

She had to set her mind to something else. Why not a Dreamtime series of children's books? That seemed like a good idea. Her style was particularly adapted to magical themes.

Matt Howarth, his hazel eyes like stones, was sitting in the back seat of the second 4WD cursing his luck. This wasn't going a bit the way he intended. Up front Dave and Sunderland's beautiful iceberg of a sister were working their way through a whole range of subjects, Dave's travels, his shock encounter with a drug lord, her encounter with a ruthless tycoon who gave every appearance of wanting to separate her from her husband but definitely wasn't Robert Redford, what was happening around the globe, what governments were going to do about it, Dave even told her stories from when he'd started out as a photographer filming interiors for which he'd been in great demand, then gardens, even food. He'd done a stint for a well-known gourmet magazine. They appeared to be getting on famously, whereas he was locked into a sickening bout of jealousy. Being separated from Sam was like a slap in the face to him.

From time to time they tried to include him in the conversation but his responses were such they must have concluded he was finding the humid heat enervating. Dave's glance was even a bit *anxious*. Dave was a kindly guy, but then he had seen and photographed so much human suffering. It had had its effect. Dave championed the underdog, the underprivileged, the downtrodden. Just when he thought he'd been presented with a marvellous opportunity to launch his campaign for winning Samantha over, along came the Great White Hunter with his bloody commanding height and film star good looks. And those assessing light eyes. Who had eyes that colour apart from his sister? Matt had the distinct impression Sunderland was trying to split him and Sam apart. Did he want her himself? The very thought turned his stomach.

The whole thing looked like being intolerable. The dynamics were all different having Sutherland along. Matt's resentments festered. He'd confidently expected he and Sam would be sharing the back seat instead just as Sam went to slide in beside him giving him the most delicious shivers of anticipation, Sunderland had cut in coolly, without waiting for her reply:

"You're riding with me."

Arrogant bastard!

His reaction had been so violent it had winded him. This was no ordinary guy like he'd been expecting. Tough, yes, but a bit of a bush whacker. No such luck! The cattle baron was upper crust. Everything had to be done *his* way. Lived like lords these cattle barons. It made his skin prickle with heat. They didn't act like *normal* people. They were *nobles,* no less. What they were doing was important. Anyone would think the country couldn't survive without them. So they had pioneered the Never Never. Who cared? They were rich enough weren't they in their bloody great homesteads. He wasn't going to lose Sam to any cattle baron. No, sir! He was in so deep he could never ever look at another woman again.

He'd known Sam now for a couple of years, but despite his best efforts, and reading up surreptitiously all the right things a guy should do, he was still no more than a friend. He couldn't possibly push it with Dave around. Dave doted on his little sister. Just a handful of times she'd accepted his invitations, a rock concert, cricket match, football final, race meeting, things like that. Open air, crowds, nothing remotely romantic. But he'd managed to kiss her lovely lips. Nothing more, but he'd lived on it. Was still drunk on it for that matter. She was an angel with that glorious exuberant mane of hair. But Sam seemed to place a higher value on him as a friend and her brother's assistant than a would-be suitor. What would she think if she knew he had taken hundred of photographs of her? Most of them when she didn't even know he was around. Some people might think he was a stalker but he wasn't. He was deeply in love with her. The last thing in the world he meant Sam was harm. Why the walls of his apartment were decorated with beautiful shots of her, walking, talking, laughing, pensive, huge blow-ups of her lovely face, so ripe and alive begging for him to touch her. She had such a luscious mouth under that small pert nose. Technically he supposed the woman in the front passenger seat, the Great White Hunter's sister, was more beautiful, but her features had the remote perfection of a classical statue. The black hair and the ice-aqua eyes only served to complete the picture. Give him Samantha's ever changing expressions, her wonderful *bright* colouring every time. For all her nice manners and upper class voice he thought the rumours about Isabelle Hartmann were bound to be true. Her husband was reputed to have been a very nice guy not some dissolute playboy. You wouldn't have to look too closely to see she was a cold bitch underneath. He knew from experience women found Dave absolutely charming. He could *reach* them somehow. He was certainly getting a response from the Snow Queen.

Buy hey, *he* was attractive to women too. Don't let's forget that. He dressed well, worked out, was nice looking, mannerly, thoughtful. He'd had a pretty lousy time of it going back a bit, but he was climbing the ladder. He was no loser. He could have lots of girls if he wanted but the truth was Sam had ruined him for the rest. His mother—he took good care to keep away from *her*—always said he had an obsessive nature as though that was something for her to worry about. Why not obsess when you had something to obsess about? It meant he was wonderfully *loyal*.

He had a lot of time for Dave. Dave was a good bloke. He'd been very good to him, very supportive after his layoff—a slight breakdown actually—call it what you like. They'd overworked him at the TV channel not that he'd shed any tears over getting the sack. Pompous old McCutcheon had a spot of abuse coming. He had explained it all to Dave who gave him a chance. He had a B.A. in photography not that he was one to boast. Surely Dave would welcome him as a brother-in-law? He would love Sam as she had never been loved. Work hard to keep her safe. She was so lovely, *lovely*. With Sam he knew he could become as steady as a rock.

CHAPTER FIVE

FROM long experience Samantha knew her brother would go to any lengths to get the shots he wanted. He was the *true* professional dedicated to his craft which he had turned into *art*. She also knew he took no account of fatigue, hunger, intense heat, even personal danger. Over the next two days she and Isabelle were left alone for hours while the men went in search of sites Ross Sunderland and Joe Goolatta brooded over before pronouncing it too arduous a trek for the women especially in the steamy heat.

"He's treating us like cream puffs," Samantha fumed.

"Maybe a little bit," Isabelle conceded. "But you wouldn't enjoy trekking through the mangroves which is where they're heading today. The mozzies are merciless. They'd *love* your skin. And mine. Don't forget it's a place where the crocs still attack but they'll be extra careful. Joe has a thing going with the crocs. That's his totem. Don't fret. We'll see plenty."

"I've already seen plenty," Samantha responded, suddenly repentant. "In fact I'm immensely grateful I'm here. And it's all due to you. Your dear brother would never have taken me."

Isabelle smiled at the sarcasm. She could see the way Ross and Samantha struck sparks from each other and she wasn't unhappy about it. "I think you've shown him you're made of the right stuff." A little pause. "Would it be presumptuous of me to ask if you and Matt have a history?"

Samantha gasped. "Honest answer?"

"Please."

"No." Samantha slapped at an insect. "I've known Matt for as long as he's been David's assistant. He lectures at an adult learning college at night and he does private photographic work. Weddings, studio portraits that sort of thing. David told me Matt had a breakdown a few years back. Overwork, lost opportunities, hassles with his superior at work. Matt doesn't talk about it. Especially not to me. He likes to present himself as a guy who's getting it all together."

Sitting beside Samantha beneath a shade tree a little distance from the camp, Isabelle turned to her. "You know he's in love with you?"

Samantha groaned. "Oh, don't say that!" Isabelle was quite right and she'd have to face it.

"Surely you know?" Isabelle asked quietly, alerted by something in Matt's manner. Something secretive. Something hidden. She knew all about manic upsurges in men. Matt harboured resentments, though on the surface he tried hard to be pleasant. "He never takes his eyes off you." Isabelle made the judgement from the depths of her own bitter experience.

Samantha sighed deeply. "That sounds like a warning, Isabelle. I haven't given Matt any reason to believe we could become more than friends."

"Does he need a reason?"

"Probably not being what we are. Is something worrying you, Isabelle?" For that matter Samantha had noticed Matt never looked at Ross with liking though his responses were courteous enough.

"D'you think he's becoming a little jealous?"

Samantha flushed. "Of Ross?"

Isabelle nodded. "He's very edgy when Ross is around. They're so different in style. In fact a complete contrast. Ross and David had instant rapport which has only grown, but it's not the same with Matt. It seems to me he's increasingly looking for conflict where there is none. He has to be *needed*. Some men are like that." A remembering chill struck her bones. "I could be overstating it but it seems to me Matt's starting to act as if he's being left out."

Spot on. "And you think it's because of me?" Samantha asked unhappily.

"Well you're the one he cares about. He was very peevish wouldn't you say last night when you and Ross dropped the sparring and carried on the conversation in perfect accord." In fact to Isabelle's discerning eyes jealousy had been coming off him in waves.

Samantha made a little grimace. "Well for all our little clashes, I agree with Ross about so many issues. However, I did notice Matt had his nose out of joint. I don't know what I can do about it though."

"Be on your guard," Isabelle suggested. "I don't mean to suggest for a minute Matt could present a danger, but maybe a little problem. Being included in David's book is important to him, I know. He wouldn't want to do anything to jeopardize that." She leant forward to retrieve the coffee mugs she had laid on the ground. "What about if you and I do a little exploring on our own, this afternoon?"

"And risk the Boss Man's ire?" Samantha asked blithely.

"So that's what you call him?" Isabelle looked across with a smile.

"And don't you dare tell him," Samantha said, scrambling to her feet. "I haven't got a way with your brother, have I?"

"Really?" Isabelle raised an arched brow. "I thought you *had*."

Which was precisely what was putting Matt Howarth's nose out of joint.

The afternoon's rigours gave Samantha a hearty appetite. The men returned full of the day's exploits. Or rather Ross and David talked as if they'd had a glorious time, thoroughly successful, while Matt's chief concern was his mosquito bites which were giving him noticeable gip.

"You'll have to stop scratching, Matt, you could get a secondary infection. I've got a good hydrocortisone cream I can give you," Samantha tried to console him. "As a matter of fact I'll get it now. See any crocs today?" she asked, as they walked to the tent she and Isabelle shared.

"Plenty," he grunted finding it difficult to control his feelings. "I couldn't wait to get the hell out of there." He gave a genuine shudder, his terror still not evaporated. "Sunderland dragged us through the swamps. They're overflowing with everything. Dank and steamy with awful muddy soil, snakes and all kinds of insects and tree roots that are only there to trip you up. By the time it was all over I could have yelled bloody murder."

"But isn't that what David wanted? The swamps may be difficult and dangerous but they're the central element in the coastal ecosystem. I bet he took some wonderful shots. I know my brother. He comes up with something entirely different from the pack. That's why he's famous. It's the special way *he* sees things."

He grasped her arm, detaining her. "David is *my* friend."

Samantha disengaged herself, feeling dismayed. "Of course he is. What's the matter, Matt. We're only a few days into the trip yet you seem right out of sorts. I thought you were really going to enjoy this trip. I'm loving it and we've travelled a long way for it. It's not too late to go back if you feel so strongly. I daresay we can manage with one vehicle."

That she could say such a thing caused him physical pain. "Is that what you want, for me to *disappear?*" To his horror, his voice broke.

"Listen, Matt, today upset you. I can see that. But you'll have to settle down. Ross is looking this way."

"To hell with Ross!" Matt exploded, his heart thumping wildly. "Is that supposed to make me cringe?"

Samantha walked on, anxiety flooding her. "I don't want to see you lose control, Matt. I thought you were going to be as excited about this as the rest of us."

"Excited?" His tone leapt. "You wouldn't feel so excited if you'd been eaten alive by mozzies. They're as big as helicopters."

"I'm sorry. So sorry," Samantha said gently. "Wait here a moment and I'll get the cream."

Instead of waiting as she asked, he pushed into the tent behind her. "What was really exciting me, Sam, was the opportunity for you and me to be together."

Studying his tormented face Samantha felt the last thing she could do was humiliate him. "Matt, dear, aren't we comfortable being friends?"

"You know I want more," he said passionately, reached out for her arm.

Why have I realised too late where all this was going, Samantha thought wretchedly. "Friendship is all I can offer, Matt," she said with great compassion.

Incredibly he began to laugh. "It's Sunderland isn't it? I've got eyes. I can see. The two of you keep up the sparring, but it's only a smoke screen for something else."

"You're talking nonsense, Matt," Samantha took a step backwards. This was a Matt she had never seen.

"I think not." His eyes were liquid with emotion. "Just don't forget in a very short while he'll be out of the picture altogether, the arrogant bastard."

Samantha counted ten before she answered. "I think you're mistaking a natural superiority—he is after all, a high achiever—for arrogance. You see him with Joe. Would an arrogant white man treat an aboriginal employee like *family?* I don't think so. Anyway why don't you take it up with him, Matt?" Samantha swooped on the cream which mercifully was to hand and passed it to him. "I hope this helps."

He realised too late he had overplayed his hand. His only option was to act out remorse. "I'm sorry, Sam." He hung his head contritely. "Of course I'm not being fair. He's Someone, even I can see that… But if you could just give me a chance?"

Samantha stood there pitying, but adamant. "You're my

friend, Matt. I'm sorry, but I can't offer anything else. The others will be waiting for us. We'd better go." She went to brush past him but he startled her by caching her around the waist.

"*Please,* Sam."

In the blink of an eye he felt like he *hated* her.

Sensing something was not *right* Samantha twisted away.

"Everything okay here?" a vibrant voice asked.

In the opening of the igloo like tent stood a tall, muscular figure caught in a freeze frame. Ross ducked his dark head and stepped inside, the glow from the gas lamps throwing his shadow high on the nylon mesh side. In that confined area—roughly one hundred square feet—generous enough for a two-person tent, he appeared quite dramatically larger than life.

Samantha had never been so glad to see anyone. "We were just coming," she said, taking a few swift paces towards him like he was her saviour. "I gave Matt some cream for his mosquito bites."

Sunderland continued to stand with his tall shadow on the wall. "They wouldn't have been nearly so bad, Matt, had you used the spray I offered you this morning." He stood aside so Samantha could exit the tent. "Next time you'll use it."

A seething reply rose to Matt's lips, but he bit it off. Much as he disliked him, Sunderland wasn't the man to tangle with. Matt too left the tent, stalking off towards where the others were seated around the camp fire. Fury at Sunderland's reprimand was burning in his chest.

"What was that all about?" Ross asked, letting his flashlight play along the ground ahead of where they walked. They were using a small petrol driven generator out of the back of one of the vehicles to cast additional light on the site, but the bush was blacker than black at night.

Samantha didn't want to tell him. She had to *think*. "He's a bit upset. He's a sensitive soul, Matt."

Sunderland just laughed. "Don't you think it's time for him to grow up?"

"Don't be impatient with him. He hasn't had your upbring-ing. His skin is quite fair. I've seen the bites. He must feel on fire."

"Well I'm sorry about that," Ross said, not even bothering to disguise the impatience in his voice, "but I'm afraid Matt point-edly chose to ignore my advice this morning when David and I were sensibly giving ourselves a good protective dousing."

Samantha walking at his shoulder, was vividly aware of his physical *presence*. It was something that could not be ignored, or locked away for when she was on her own. *I've regressed to adoring teenager with an almighty crush.* "I can't understand why Matt was so foolish. He's not usually like that."

"Are you sure you really know him?" Ross asked, his voice dry. "Or just vaguely?"

"I know him well enough." It wasn't the right answer. She only *thought* she knew him.

"You'd tell me if he started to bother you?" He paused as they came within the perimeter of light. It was marvellous the way she kept so shiningly clean and fresh even when tramping through the bush in the humid heat. "Certainly you would tell David?"

Her eyes remained focused on him as though she were un-able to look away. Her whole being seemed to be *melting* so powerful was his attraction. "Matt won't do anything to wreck his chances with David. Matt's not really a man of action, I sup-pose." She sounded distressed. "Being out of his element has made him feel inadequate, but he'll pick up."

"So how come *you* don't act helpless?"

"I want to impress you," she said lightly when she was speaking the exact truth. "Prove what I can do. Stuff like that."

"You're managing to get away with it too," he commented dryly as though admitting to a weakness. "As for Matt, he knew what he was in for surely?"

"Give him a chance, Ross," she pleaded.

God, the use of his name packed a punch. He clenched his fists before he surrendered to the dangerous impulses that pow-ered through him; to pull her into his arms. Every minute he was with her, the desire to do so grew. Tonight that feeling was tremendously strong. Still he managed to keep his tone businesslike. "Certainly I'll give him a chance, if only because you champion him so sweetly." He made sure she heard the sarcasm. "I don't want to get on his case, but I have to tell you after today David isn't too far off telling him to straighten up his act." He avoided saying Howarth had never let up whining for most of the afternoon until at one point he nearly gave into the urge to chuck him in the swamp. He knew Howarth had problems. Even his devotion to Samantha was a little creepy in character. He changed the subject to something less stressful. "So you and Belle went hiking this afternoon?"

She looked up at him with a smile. "We had a wonderful time. It's very powerful country and it's having its effect on me. Isabelle is an excellent guide in her own right and such good company."

"She says the same of you. I'm very grateful you and Belle are getting on so well. She's had a great grief to cope with but she's got the courage to rise above it given enough time. *I* was the one who got it wrong. Your coming along as it turns out, Ms Langdon, was a great idea."

"Momentous words!" she crowed. "See how *easy* it was to say them?"

"Well I'm not suggesting you move into my tent."

Her heart jumped. "Don't you play your games with me."

"Oh?" He sent her a sizzling glance. "It hasn't crossed your mind?"

"Oh, all right it has, but I'm not about to admit to it. Mercifully I can control my feelings."

"But you've just admitted to having them?"

"Which is more than I can say for you. You're *deep*, Boss Man. Impossibly deep. In fact you're a dangerous man."

"Now how would *you* know?"

How beautiful he was! She could sit and stare at him for ages.

"I know." She said with fervour.

"Do you now. I would never hurt you. Your boyfriend is more likely to do that than me. I have to tell you I'm keeping a watchful eye on him."

"Hold on a bit." She was dismayed. "I can handle Matt. Okay? It's *you* I can't handle."

He stared down at her. She was wearing a cool little top with a gauzy flowered skirt that had an uneven hem that was undoubtedly the rage. Her beautiful, oh so feminine hair was pulled back into some arrangement of plaits he found very attractive, even when he wanted to set those plaits loose. "When men collapse around you like soufflés?"

Perversely she was amused and charmed. "Well not *collapse* exactly. I think you've got me down as *dangerous* as well."

He answered without hesitation. "It so happens you're *right!*"

"Do I *look* dangerous?"

"I've no intention of flattering you."

"I'd be very surprised if you did. Like you, I want reasons. You must have made some kind of decision that involvement with a woman you perceive to be unsuitable would be akin to a rope around your neck?"

Dismal scenes from his memory bank flashed up. He even remembered the way at night time his father used sometimes take the hair brush from his mother as she sat at her dressing table and proceed to draw it through her beautiful long hair, his face wearing such an expression of love. "Not to mention a giant leap into the unknown," he replied with unnecessary harshness. "Heaven for a time then a detour to hell."

She regarded him with trepidation. "You confuse me. You tell me one thing, the next you speak as from bitter experience?"

I don't want this, he thought. *I'm in thrall to this woman and I don't want to accept it. Hadn't he learned the hard way? Hadn't he been warned?*

"The moment I saw you…" He stopped dead before she prised it out of him.

"Yes?" She caught her breath as if on the brink of a revelation.

There was a recklessness in his blood he knew was getting the better of him. *Calm down,* he exhorted himself, on the fine edge of frustration. She was with him every waking minute. She had insinuated herself into his dreams. Certainly it was witchcraft.

In a way it was like being locked in silken chains.

He looked at her through the mask he affected. "I knew then I'd have need of protective armour." He turned away, knowing he was leaving her baffled. Why not? He never meant to say half the things he was saying. "We'd better join the others. Joe's the chef tonight."

"That's right change the subject." She had to near jog to keep up. "I'd love to know what you were really going to say."

"The fact I even said it, makes me wonder."

"It would be really something to see. *You* losing control."

"Well you're not going to see it tonight," he answered bluntly. "Tomorrow, who knows? Joe is taking Dave and Matt out on a trip of his own while I take you and Belle somewhere you'll enjoy. Maybe a swim. I know just the spot. We can get most of the way in the 4WD then we'll have to trek. A little reward for being good and not doing too much complaining."

Her dark eyes slanted up at him. "You are *such* an enigma, Ross Sunderland."

"And like a woman you're desperate to solve the mystery. Are you going to say thank you?"

"Give me a moment." She touched her temple. "It's odd to be in your good books. I'll say please *and* thank you just for good measure. In fact I appreciate the thought so much I'm nearly on the point of tears."

It was then he shocked her into absolute silence. "I can almost feel them on my tongue."

The seductive note in his voice roused her so much he might have suddenly begun to trail a hand over her body. She could feel the blood flushing her cheeks and her neck. He had to be the most perverse man she had ever known.

* * *

Dinner was freshly caught barramundi on a bed of basmati rice spiced up with ginger and chilli and a splash of lemon, served with considerable panache by Joe. It was a simple meal that became a taste sensation because of the freshness and superb flavour of the giant perch, one of the world's great eating fish and a symbol of the Territory. It really was like being on an old-style safari Samantha thought, hungry and utterly under a spell. This trip couldn't be long enough.

They ate around a collapsible table covered each evening with a fresh linen cloth and matching napkins. No plastic plates for them. Isabelle had sorted all that out at the homestead. They had good china, good stainless steel cutlery and fine wine glasses at their disposal. Peaches and cream out of tins for dessert. Good wine. Good coffee. Tremendous good will which was grating terribly on Matt's already strained nerves.

Afterwards they sat around in comfortable deck chairs that creaked as they moved, conversing lightly, enjoying the night.

How different it all was in the wild bush, Samantha thought. Like a dream. The sky over this marvellous mystical country was incredibly clear. She lay back in her chair staring raptly at the sky. The stars were like glowing windows through which poured the dazzling light of Heaven. Over the tip of a grove of spiky pandanus hung the Southern Cross. The air was blessedly cool after the heat of the day, the light breeze carrying myriad scents from the abundant wild flowers and fruits that appeared almost overnight from the heralding storms. She sniffed in the fragrance. There was a definite high note of wild gardenia and something else, not jasmine, but musky blossom. It was every-where…so soporific…. She was a woman, enchanted. Liberated from the everyday world.

"You're drifting off," a voice close to her ear brought her out of her reverie.

Samantha's eyes flew open. She stared up at Ross, fantasising what it would be like to be here with him alone. She was already in love with him. Had been from the moment he had pinned her with those extraordinary eyes. It owed nothing to the time or the place though that added to the magic. She knew beyond all possible doubt this was no easy thing. She could be badly hurt. "Now you know I don't snore," she covered the fierce spasms of yearning with the mundane.

He lowered himself to the rug at her feet, drawing up his long legs. "No, but you talk in your sleep."

"What?" She leaned over the better to see his handsome face. "You've really heard me?"

He made a soft, scoffing sound. "Actually it's more like a mumble."

"So you've been spying on me? Is that what you're saying?"

"Do you want me to spy on you?" He glanced up at her.

"I'd never feel safe."

"Well relax. I check on the tents and the perimeter of the camp last thing at night before I hit the hay myself."

"Oh." She relaxed. "You had me going for a minute. Clearly you have your responsibilities." She lay back, her hands behind her head, feeling so *wired* it was a wonder she wasn't lit up. "You know what I'd *really* like to do?"

Even in the semidark she could see the sparkle of his eyes. "Join me on the rug?"

He was doing it again. Trying to throw her off balance. It shouldn't be allowed. A blush rushed over her skin. "I'm much too cautious to do that."

"What do you think might happen?" *I mightn't be able to get enough of you?*

"Absolutely nothing," she responded to his half derisive tone. "And just to prove it." She lowered herself onto the rug, but keeping a foot away from him. "Besides, the eyes of the world are on us."

"Really?" He turned his dark head. Joe was moving about, obviously making preparations for the morning. Matt was no-where in sight. Gone off to bed in a huff without saying good-night? David and Belle were sitting companionably side by side, David's tawny head bent to Isabelle's sable, as he passed some remark which was met by a soft burst of laughter. They shared an affinity which was plain to see. Belle was glowing, absorbed. She seemed to have thrown off the grinding grief. Beyond that Ross could think no further.

"No one's taking the slightest notice of us," he pointed out. "We could disappear into the jungle if we liked."

"To do what?" Excitement moved in with a great rush of wings.

He trapped her gaze. "I think it would be fair to say, Samantha, I was attracted to you from the start." Why deny what was in the very air? If he admitted the attraction he might be able to head it off.

The admission had her incandescent. "Someone should have told me. You acted like you disliked me on sight."

He reached out and grasped her hand, that now lay at her side, lightly twining her fingers through his own. "That's a lie, Samantha." The urge to pull her closer was so overwhelming he almost forgot where he was, who he was, *everything!* He'd tried so hard to fight this feeling of losing himself. He was too accustomed, too comfortable with control. His male territory. Except since he met her he was a different man.

No wonder men went mad about women, he thought, for the first time totally comprehending his father's dilemma. She was staring at him with her large eyes, her bright copper hair now unconfined, splashing over her bare creamy shoulders and curving to her breast. Her woman's fragrance, fresh, natural, hauntingly sweet all around them, flooding him with desire. He could feel the heavenly softness and texture of her skin. It was like satin against the roughness of his work hardened hands.

"Ross?"

His mouth twisted. He released her hand, grateful in a way he could still do that. "You sound like a little girl frightened of the dark."

"I'm more afraid of *you*." She continued to look directly at him, trying to reconcile the barrage of contradictory messages he was sending. "What is it you're trying to do?"

"God knows!" His voice cracked. "Lose myself for a while." *Pin your warm, beautiful, living body to the ground. Kiss your lovely mouth. Unbutton your shirt. Let my hand find your naked breasts. Immerse myself in you.*

Hot blood was like a swirling darkness before his eyes. The force of his desire for her was getting worse with every passing day. Lord knows he had tried to put up defences. They didn't work. Somehow without his wanting it, she had slid in behind his heart. He had learned the worst way possible there was terror in wanting a woman so much. Did that tearing, violent, disruptive desire last or slip away? It had lasted with his father. He had the underlying conviction it would last with him.

Was that a blessing or a disaster? Though he would never act with the quietness and resignation of his father. He had a far more combative nature. He'd have gone to England and dragged his wife home. Kicking and screaming if he had to. Vows were vows. Marriage wasn't a sport, a recreation. Marriage was total commitment. The children of a marriage had to be protected. Did his mother have any *real* idea of the suffering she had caused or was she now full of regrets? I hope so, he thought with anguish. What she had done deserved punishment.

Watching him Samantha shivered. "You look so grim. What are you thinking?"

He bowed his head. "A hell of a long way back."

"Do you want to talk about it?"

"No," he said bleakly. "It's not as though you could come up with a solution. It's all gone well beyond that." He stood up resolutely, giving her his hand. "A reasonably early night might be a good idea. I'll have a word with David before we turn in."

Once on her feet, she had a sudden hysterical desire to wrap her arms around him; lay her head against his chest. But she had her pride. "Does Isabelle know we're going with you?" she asked quietly.

"I'm sure David has told her by now." He had returned to his clipped tone. "It was meant to be a surprise, but there's such accord between them."

"Aren't you glad?" she asked gravely.

A muscle jumped along his clean sculpted jawline. "As far as it's going, yes."

"Isn't that a matter for them?"

"Belle is mourning her husband, Samantha."

Samantha had qualms she couldn't even put her finger on. "I know. Forgive me if I sound insensitive. I'm not suggesting for a moment it could be easy, but Isabelle has to survive the terrible blow that life inflicted on her. Her husband has gone and no amount of crying will bring him back. The agony must be extreme. She told me she's been numb with it. But she's so young and so beautiful. Isabelle has decades and decades in front of her. You wouldn't want her to be *alone?* It can't be easy for a woman alone. Moreover a woman who has no children. I have learned from Isabelle she loves kids."

"Do *you?*" His face was in deep shadow but his voice was intense.

"I know exactly how many children I want. I want four."

"*One* husband?"

"Of course one husband. Isn't that what every woman wants when she goes into marriage?"

"I hate to remind you your parents divorced."

She sighed deeply. "They had to. It was too painful for them to remain together. Actually it was my father who was unfaithful. He was the real culprit. Divorce was the last thing my mother wanted, but after all the cruelties and humiliations, no longer loved, betrayed, rejected, she became so bitter and angry I think she wanted to kill my father. And his mistress."

Your poor bloody father is trying to recover his lost youth! Her mother had never run out of that explanation.

Samantha shut down on her old memories. She was very good at it from long habit.

"It's a mean old world out there," Ross said. "There are some wounds the soul can never recover from."

Samantha looked up at the blossoming stars as though seeking answers. One blazed down the sky leaving a trail of white fire. She made a wish. That she would be granted the priceless gift of finding her true love. Her soul mate. "Perhaps if one is patient and lets the anger go instead of holding on to it," she suggested, and surprised herself by taking his arm. She wasn't rejected. He drew her close to his side. "I believe recovery *is* possible, Ross. In the meantime we have to take comfort where we can. Somehow David is shielding Isabelle from the worst of her sorrow. We can only be grateful for that."

They were settled comfortably for the night before Isabelle whispered into the semi-darkness. "You're happy about going off on your own with Ross tomorrow?" In the course of talking over the following day's itinerary, between them they had come up with a change of plan that seemed to suit everyone. Isabelle was now to join David's party. Samantha was to go with Ross.

Samantha levered herself up onto one elbow. Happy? The truth of it was she was ecstatic. "I'd say it's shaping up to be one of the highlights of my life," she whispered back. "You engineered it, didn't you, you designing woman?"

Isabelle cut her laugh short. The night was so *quiet* and voices carried. "I have to confess seeing you both together has aroused my matchmaking talents."

"What? You're not joking?"

"Oh, Sam, I have eyes. Besides, I know my brother. I know the flash of his eyes. Underneath the formidable exterior he's passionate and emotional."

"With me, he's mostly an enigma," Samantha sighed, lying back and settling her head into the small pillow. "It's scary being struck by lightning."

"Is that what it feels like?" Isabelle asked gently.

"It's a wonder I haven't been hospitalised," Samantha remarked wryly. "I'm way out of my depth here, Isabelle. Your brother is very very suspicious of me."

"Hang in there," Isabelle advised in a sisterly way. "It's not surprising you know given our history. Our mother bolted. She didn't set a good precedent for the female sex. For what it's worth, there's no one I'd rather see my brother taking such an interest in. It's just that Ross over the years has become accustomed to being the man in control. He's very disciplined. That means he doesn't lose his head over women and he's had a lot literally throw themselves at him. I've seen it with my own eyes. Even when he's been with another girl, they take no notice. Shameless. Ross has seen a lot of failed relationships. So have I. So have you. You suffered similarly when your parents divorced and that must have been very hard. Ross worshipped Dad and Dad had such pride in him. Ross is extremely hostile to our mother for what she did not only to us but mostly what she did to Dad. It's made him very wary because if he weren't he could star in a replay of Dad's life. You know about emotional wreckage. God knows I do. Ross had been programmed to fight becoming enmeshed with a woman who really got under his skin and you pretty much have."

Samantha turned her head to where Isabelle was lying. "You wouldn't say that if you didn't believe it."

Isabelle just smiled. "And why not? You have a lot going for you."

"We both do. You and me. But I can't hide the fact I feel very vulnerable where Ross is concerned."

"We're all vulnerable," Isabelle reminded her, backing away from dangerous ground.

"He could forget me in a week." Samantha mused, gazing at the big copper moon through the screened window in the side of the tent. There was one opposite allowing cross ventilation.

"Could *you* forget him?"

Samantha was lost for a moment trying to think how she could adjust to a life without Ross Sunderland in it. "Not if a thousand years went past."

"Well then!" Isabelle smiled in the darkness.

"So are *you* happy going with David's party?" Samantha asked, buoyed up by Isabelle's approval.

"Yes of course." Isabelle tried to convey no more than easy acceptance when each minute in David's company she was re-awakening to the richness of life. "Actually I'm not completely responsible for the change of plan. David wants to include me in some of his shots."

"The human figure in the vast landscape?"

"Yes. He's wanting shots of you as well."

"I have to get the text right. That's important and my head is already swimming with ideas." Samantha gave a light yawn, finding the scent of the woodsmoke from the fire intoxicating. "The ones David's taken on the digital camera are great. I can't wait to see the film scanned. I'm going to have my pick of the digitals blown up to whatever size I want in Darwin. By the way, what happened to Matt? He just disappeared."

"He sat for a while," Isabelle murmured, quite at peace. "Then he announced rather shortly he wanted to crash. I don't think anything is working in the way Matt wanted. He's very tense and he's really feeling the heat."

"Obviously he doesn't like life stripped down to essentials," Samantha lamented. "Matt's a city person."

They both knew that wasn't the cause of Matt's ill humour.

"Belle?" Samantha whispered as Isabelle turned on her side.

"Yes?"

"Thank you for everything. You're wise and kind. I'm really glad we met. When it doesn't hurt so much to talk about what has happened to you, I'll be around to listen."

Tears stung Isabelle's eyes at the touching note in Samantha's voice. She swallowed down a sudden flare of pain. Not a lot of people had been kind to her since Blair. She knew for some bereaved people talking would be a release. But there was no talking about her marriage. The very last thing she wanted was to go back.

CHAPTER SIX

STILL smouldering in silent fury over Samantha's lack of trust in him, Matt assumed a nonchalant demeanour, strolling over to where she was down on her haunches re-arranging her pack.

"Hi, all set?" She looked so beautiful it broke his heart.

"Just about." She looked up and tried a warm smile. She knew Matt well enough to know he was feigning good humour. He didn't look well. The dark shadows beneath his eyes gave him an exhausted look as if he weren't getting enough sleep. "I hope you get the shots you want today. I can't wait to see them," she added, injecting enthusiasm into her voice.

"So far so good." He shrugged. "Of course I haven't got Dave's masterly skills. The stuff he's done so far is going to be pretty damned marvellous."

"You haven't had David's experience," she said kindly. "You're a very good photographer, Matt. You're exceptionally lucky to have Joe along with you. He knows this place like the back of his hand. Incredible to believe his people have lived in this region for more than forty thousand years ago."

"They can have it," Matt was sufficiently derailed to say.

Samantha stood up. "You can't mean that? It's marvellous and we've only experienced a little. I can't wait until we get to see the rock art. It's considered to be without parallel in all the world."

"Yes, yes, I know." Now Matt's irritation was barely disguised. "Whose idea was it for you to go off with Sunderland?"

Samantha tried to rein her temper in. "I'm tempted to say mine, Matt. Actually Ross was to take Belle and me but David wanted the human element in some of his shots so he invited Belle along. Surely you know?"

He didn't even attempt an answer. "You two get along well?"

"Belle and I?"

"She doesn't strike me as the grieving widow," he said in a bitterly sarcastic voice.

Tenderhearted Samantha was greatly distressed. "What a rotten thing to say."

"Is it?" Matt's brown head was poised curiously like a cobra's about to strike. "Word is she drove the poor man to his death."

"Oh Matt!" Samantha dropped the tin mug in her hand. It hit the ground and rolled away. "That I do *not* believe. I'd advise you not to listen to cruel rumours. A woman as beautiful as Isabelle is always the target for vicious gossip. That's the way of the world. Usually it's other women. Not *men* so much."

"Okay I'm sorry." Matt dropped his head, pretending shame. "But take a look at her when she's laughing with Dave. I'm convinced she's got him lined up as her next."

"We need the Davids of this world," Samantha said sharply. "Lucky for you he was around when your life was in the doldrums. Isabelle is suffering. David is trying to ease her pain. I don't know what's got into you, Matt. Your health doesn't seem so good. Since we left Darwin you seem to have lost your sense of well-being."

"Why not!" he exploded, yearning to show her how much he loved her. He'd fight a duel over her if he had to only that bastard, Sunderland, would win. Sunderland, the natural born leader accepting adulation as his due. "Everything has turned out so differently from what I expected," he said. It made him furious. He hated it. "I'm trying. I'm trying the best I can. What would be really great is if you and I could get to spend a little time together. That would be wonderful, just the two of us."

Samantha wanted to end this, but was torn by pity. "We share breakfast and dinner, Matt. We get to relax around the camp fire. It's *you* who doesn't want to join in."

Matt set his fine white teeth together. "I'm talking about spending a little time *alone*," he ground out. "You're spending the day with the Great White Hunter. Why not me? No one could enjoy your company better. We've always had a great time when we've been out, haven't we?"

"Of course we have. We're friends. If you don't see it that way, I've told you, Matt. I can't offer anything more."

"Because you've fallen for Sunderland," Matt muttered like he had a score to settle.

"How come you know more than I do, Matt?" Samantha tried to take the heat off Ross. "You know the way it works. Ross is our guide. And he's coming this way. It's about time we all got going."

Matt's hazel eyes held hers, something desperate in his thin face. "All I want from you is only what you're prepared to offer. I care about you, Sam. Remember that. All I'm asking of you is to come with me while *I* take a few photographs. I'm far more interested in photographing you than the scenery. Is that so much to ask?"

"No of course not!" Samantha tried to mollify him.

"Great!" Matt smacked his fist into his palm, a triumphant look on his face.

Ross and Samantha drove across flood plains rejuvenated by the tropical storms that had already started. Mostly they occurred in the afternoon, short lived, maybe thirty or forty minutes, but spectacular enough. It was the late night thunderstorms that turned on the most awesome displays of Nature's unmatched power. Once the Wet really got underway, January was the worst month, access to many areas of the park became too dangerous to attempt. As it was these same plains they were travelling over would be inundated and the Park's innumerable water lily covered lagoons and billabongs would become home to the legions of beautiful wading birds that returned from Asia to the lush grasslands.

Ross pulled over under a magnificently gnarled paperbark, scattering the masses of brilliantly coloured parrots that were resting in the willowy, iridescent branches. Birds and birdsong was everywhere all over the Park. Parrots, cockatoos, lorikeets, galahs, corellas, rosellas, warblers, honeyeaters. There were even plenty of the great flightless bird, the emu.

He cut the ignition. "Right!" His sparkling gaze swept her, the large velvety eyes, the creamy skin the flushed cheeks. With her beautiful hair bound up in plaits she looked about sixteen and crying out to be kissed. "Our trek starts here. Still up for it?"

She answered readily. "I'm game if you are, Captain."

"Yes, well, we haven't started yet."

"Give me two seconds." She opened out the passenger door and slid to the ground. "Tell me where we're heading. Point it out," she challenged, well and truly on her mettle.

His amusement was apparent. "See that small range?" he walked around the back of the vehicle to join her.

She almost reeled. "Gosh, I could hardly miss it." Her eyes travelled to a flat escarpment washed with purple against the smouldering blue sky. "It must be twenty miles away."

He made a soft jeering sound. "That's a lousy guess. It's closer to five. No more than my daily constitutional. Anyway, you said you wouldn't miss this for the world."

She looked up at him, heroic figure that he was. "Okay let's make a start," she said briskly, easing the straps of her backpack.

"This is the *easy* bit," he assured her.

"It's time I showed you a thing or two!"

It was all he could do not to seize her and demand she prove it. "I sure am willing to learn."

"You don't think much of women, do you?" she called over her shoulder, stepping off.

His mouth twisted in a cynical smile. "Believe me I know how powerful you are. Maybe not in the physical stakes."

"That's why women last a heck of a lot longer than men." She retaliated.

"You're not killing me off, Samantha, thank you very much. What was Howarth griping about this time?" He caught her up easily, so they could walk side by side.

"Aren't you jumping to conclusions?"

"No," he answered flatly. "You *have* to tell him he has no chance with you."

"Why don't you tell him," she challenged. *He won't listen to me.*

"He's madly in love with you." He shook his dark head in disgust.

"There must be worse things in life," she said tartly.

"Not for your friend, Matt. I could be wrong but he strikes me as a man on the verge of a break-down."

Samantha let out a long sigh, thinking there was something in what he said. "That's a bit extreme, isn't it?"

"He has the signs all over him."

She had taken note of the fevered tension. "I have told Matt I can't offer him more than friendship."

"Even that's too much," he said rather curtly. "It gives him hope."

"So what do you want me to say?" She stopped so abruptly she almost slammed into him. "I'm having an affair with you?"

His eyes gleamed, pure aquamarine. "Well, aren't you?"

"Give me a break!" she spluttered. "You're arrogant beyond belief."

That made him smile. "Don't get too steamed up. Save your strength for the trek ahead."

She stared fixedly through the lace work of trees. Most were tall palms, stands of pandanus, paperbarks, an understorey of blossoming grevilleas, native hibiscus, cassias which produced colourful scented flowers, luminous green mosses, surprisingly delicate ferns, long trailing vines, a lot bearing trumpet like flowers in cerise and purple with bright yellow centres. Not so bad. She could go a mile or two in bush like this. The land was level pegging. "Look why don't we cut this battle of the sexes short. I can do this on my own. At least to the escarpment. I've been bush walking plenty of times. You must have noticed by now how fit I am?"

They were walking so close together, their hands were almost brushing. "We're not talking a delightful stroll along a State Forest track. You're in the presence of the greatest wilderness on the continent except maybe for tropical Queensland's Cape York. Even David arranged for a guide."

"You think I'd get lost?" she asked tartly, his superior male attitude doubling her determination.

"I *know* you would."

"This isn't jungle. It's relatively open woodland. All I need to do is follow my nose to the escarpment. God knows it's smack bang in the middle. I'm determined to do this, Ross."

"What if I don't let you?" He moved with catlike grace to bar her way.

"Excuse me. I was brought up in a feuding family and survived."

He glanced around them. "Ah well, if that's the case, I might sit down for a half an hour. Give you a headstart." He eased his lean powerful body onto a large boulder, one of a rocky outcrop, that was so much a feature of the landscape. Its base was framed by emerald spear grasses. "Do you want the rifle?" he asked.

She gave an involuntary shudder. "What would I do with it? Set my sights on you? I don't even know how to hold it. No, I don't want the rifle. As long as there aren't any crocs trying to waddle up on me, I'll watch where I plant my feet."

He tilted his Akubra further down over his eyes. "All right then," he said in a relaxed accommodating fashion. "Off you go. If you're feeling disoriented or you run into any trouble just yell like hell. I'll come running."

"I'd prefer if you came driving. At top speed."

"No can do." He crossed his long outstretched legs at the ankle. "One thing you *look* the part." His eyes swept her from head to foot. She was wearing good solid walking shoes, cotton shirt and cotton jeans. On her head she wore a big floppy natural straw hat that dangled chiffon folds she could tie around her neck and even over her face in case of an insect attack.

"Well so long," she said crisply, trying to look like a professional safari goer. "See you in a couple of hours."

"Take your time," he responded pleasantly, easing off his backpack as though *he* had all the time in the world.

For more than an hour she wandered rather than tramped through the wilderness always keeping the table topped summit of the escarpment in sight. The huge diversity of flora was amazing; the great variety of fruits and nuts and gourds which almost exclusively had made up the aboriginal diet. Up ahead she could see the distinctive ghost gums with their shimmering white trunks. Joe had told her Kakadu had species of eucalypts which had never been found elsewhere. She was longing to get to the wetter areas of the park where gorgeous waterlilies wove a carpet across the dark green waters. That was a classic image of Kakadu, the great sheets of water floating their cargo of huge lily pads and exquisite blooms.

The ground cover was becoming heavier, the vines sometimes tripping her up. She saw many many birds but no mammals. They had to be asleep in their hollows. The sun wasn't too hot beneath the trees. Richly scented flowers cascaded some thirty feet down a bush giant, scarlet with cream centres. She stopped to take a closer look but didn't touch. The main reason being she didn't know what sap was poisonous and what was not. Legions of lizards scampered through the fallen tunnels of leaves. Looking up she saw, for the first time, colourful bean shaped pods growing down the barks of certain trees. Edible? She wasn't game to find out. One plentiful shrub dangled small fruit not the usual yellow, orange or bright red, but an incredible indigo blue. She wondered what it tasted like. Walking on, she tried to imagine the place when it was teeming rain. Even now it was warm, humid and *green*. Green smelling. She lifted her head to a branch of a slender tree alerted by a flash of colour.

A kingfisher with a poor little frog in its mouth. There had to be pools of water nearby. Remnants of the last flood topped up by recent storms. The kingfisher's plumage was glorious. A rich violet, bright orange breast, scarlet beak. A fallen tree probably from a lightning strike blocked her path. She would have to go around it. Now and again she had the sensation Ross Sunderland was watching her, but however swiftly she turned, eyes keen, she saw nothing. Not even a swaying frond to betray his presence. Nevertheless she had no feeling of fear or apprehension. She felt certain he was somewhere close by even if she couldn't see him.

Of course she regretted her independent stance. They should be walking through this paradise together.

Dry leaves crackled underfoot as she circled around the decaying trunk that was covered in rich fungi. She was still heading in a straight unimpeded line for the flat topped purple range. This was really the first time in her life she'd been up close and personal with a tropical wilderness. No real predators. No lions and tigers. She hadn't come to the crocs or the wallowing buffalos that did so much damage to the environment. She realised the deadly taipan lived in the Park but hardly anyone saw it. Snakes kept to themselves.

Blithely she continued her walk, imagining how marvellous it was going to be to go swimming at the end of it. Mineral springs. No crocs.

Out of the corner of her eye she saw a long black shadow detach itself from the cover of the trees.

She stood dumbstruck too petrified to move. Then, "Get. Get out of here!" She lifted her arm warningly.

The perentie, the giant goanna, fully eight feet long sheafed in speckled black and yellow chain mail ignored her, holding its frightening stance. She could feel herself shaking as if it were a crocodile. The monitor had such powerful limbs and a strong thrashing tail. Its sharp claws were dug into the track, its purple tongue extended. She knew it could run as fast as a race horse and she knew it could inflict serious wounds if threatened.

She battled to give voice to a cry, but her throat was closed and dry. Where the hell was Sunderland when she needed him?

"Get!" she croaked.

She was wasting time. A split second before the goanna decided to charge Samantha ran, heart pounding. She heaved herself up a tree, fearful the giant lizard would come after her. They climbed trees didn't they? She was mumbling to herself, inching across the branch, adrenalin pumping, hoping to God the limb would hold steady under her weight.

As she drew a tortured breath there came a sound that was stunning in the silence of the forest. A rifle shot tore into the earth a few paces from where the goanna was raised on its powerful legs, ready for battle. A second shot struck a sunken rock ricocheting away harmlessly.

Ross was beneath the tree making a furious hand signal to her to stay put.

As though she was about to disobey!

The goanna needed no more prompting. Alarmed it took off at high speed, crossing the track inches away from where Sunderland was standing, like a gun dog hell bent on retrieving a fallen bird for its master.

"You can come down now, Samantha," he called, cool as a cucumber. "Our friend has moved on."

To *joke! How dared he!* She was deaf in one ear from those shots. From being frozen with panic Samantha was incandescent with rage.

"Fall I'll catch you," he suggested, holding out his arms.

"Will you just." She launched herself through the air as though she wished to attack him only he caught her, whirling her around and around until she gasped, "Stop!" she yelled at him, kicking and lashing at him with her hands, causing them both to topple over.

She was absolutely *livid*. She wriggled on top of him, straddling him, straining to hold him down. "You rotten, mean, nasty, arrogant son of a bitch! You just stay where you are." She started to pummel him, her breath sobbing in her chest. "You *knew* chances were I might run into that monster."

"Look I'm sorry." He was absorbed in fending her off without hurting her.

"Sorry's not good enough. I've been waiting to do this for ages, you brute. You were behind me the whole time. I mightn't have been able to see you but I knew you were there."

"Top marks for having the sense to scale a tree." He caught her flailing wrists. "You did it in excellent time."

"Ross Sunderland I *hate* you!" The little gold flecks lit up her eyes.

"Let's see if you do." His look of amusement was abruptly extinguished. With one deft movement their positions were reversed. He had her pinned to the ground, looking down on her trembling body.

"Don't you dare touch me," she warned, her senses heightened to the point of pain.

He controlled her easily with one hand, but the distress in her face made him hold back the loud clamour of his own needs. Her straw hat had long since fallen off and one of her copper braids had come undone. "Now that soft growl would have done justice to a lioness," he scoffed, understanding he had to rein himself in.

"That was horrible, horrible." She shuddered. "The bloody thing was ten feet long."

"More like eight," he corrected. "They're harmless to humans unless they're threatened. She might have laid eggs close by. I'm sorry, Samantha. Really sorry. I'll let you up."

"I'll get up when I'm good and ready," she said perversely, the sensuality within not in keeping with her tart words. She studied the curve of his lips. What a beautiful mouth he had, the edges so clearly defined. She lived in hope he would kiss her the hateful beast.

"Yes, ma-am." He looked down at her, achingly aroused, but unprepared to force a response from her which he knew he could surely do. The curve of her breasts showed through the neck of her crisp blue cotton shirt. A button had come undone in their tussle, another strained to come loose. She was wearing a bikini top beneath the shirt in a much darker shade of blue. Her flesh looked so soft and creamy it begged to be fondled. He could feel the delicate weight of her breast in his hand. What it was to be filled with desire and unable to satisfy it.

"You've got no right to scare me." Her whole body was vibrant with nerves.

"Poor baby!" He wondered if the craving was showing in his eyes.

She saw it and her heart tumbled over inside of her. The unexpected tenderness brought her totally undone. Tears sparkled in her eyes.

"Don't *do* that." A muscle twitched just under his skin. His self-control had its limitations. Surely she knew? The magnetism that drew them together could be their downfall. As ever, unhappy memories were sharp and jagged in his mind. Maybe they would be there forever. Love for a woman was wonderful. And treacherous. Who could blame him for being so deeply apprehensive? This beautiful young woman was not only getting under his skin, she was cutting close to his heart. He couldn't seem to do anything to shield himself. She was the *only* one who had been able to bring the whole protective edifice down. It set off the roar in his ears and his harsh breathing. God, how he wanted her!

Samantha heard the little puff of violence in his tone; recognised the sexual hostility, that was somehow incredibly erotic.

"Let me up. It's the heat. Perspiration in my eyes." Her own fear of defencelessness made her act.

He stood up instantly, pulling her to her feet. "Maybe this time we can stick together."

"Great idea." She dusted herself off, fixed her plait and looked around for her straw hat.

He retrieved it, passing it to her. "Give me your pack."

"It's okay. I can keep up."

"*Give* it to me."

She surrendered, not all that gracefully. "Whatever you say, Boss Man."

He slipped his own pack over his shoulders. "I know you call me that."

"How do you know? I've never breathed a word."

"I can read your mind," he said crisply. "Have you anything sweet in this pack?" He began to look inside.

"Some packets of walnuts and raisins," she told him. "Why are you hungry?"

He made a quick examination of the pack, found the little cartons of dried fruit and nuts. "I'm a little concerned about *you*."

"Boy, is that a good feeling," she mocked. "Don't be too nice to me, Ross. It will go to my head."

"Okay I'll ignore you." Perversely he gave her a glance that was blindingly sensual. "Let's just get to the falls okay? I need to cool off."

CHAPTER SEVEN

CLOUDS of beautiful butterflies acted as scouts.

They were passing through an area thick with shooting grasses, pandanus showing fresh new growth and spiky low growing palms of a light green glowing colour. Yellow purple-fringed lilies and their tall upstanding leaves grew as a ground cover, so exquisite Samantha tried her level best not to step on them. It wasn't easy. The plants grew profusely. Through the light scattering of trees was the fascinating spectacle of free standing sandstone pillars, almost like people, quite different from the wedge shaped clay termite mounds she had already seen decorating the plains.

Up ahead a small tree was lit up like a beacon with large petalled flowers of a dazzling yellow. She would love to pick one.

"Listen!" Ross took her arm suddenly.

"What?" She stood perfectly still, unsure of what she was listening for. Then she heard it. "The song of the falls." She looked up at him with a beautiful smile, her face flushed, her eyes a-sparkle. "What do you call them again?"

"Ngaru. We're coming to the Ngaru lagoon, hence the birds." He pointed to the sky, as a flight of magpie geese caught the airstream. "We're almost there."

She sighed blissfully. "I can't wait for a swim. It'll be absolute *heaven!*" Though she had made no complaint—indeed she had been too enthralled with their Nature trek to think of it—she was happily exhausted. A sweat had broken out all over her, dampening her hair and causing her shirt to stick to her. She was glad now she had a fresh t-shirt rolled up in her pack which he was still carrying like it was a paper bag. He on the other hand looked like the six million dollar man. Indefatigable. Not the slightest trace of weariness. He'd have made a great explorer.

Ross took the lead as the vegetation rose up in front of them more luxuriously, parting long luminous grasses like reeds for her to tread through. Used to finding the appropriate words, she thought the wild beauty of their trek was beyond her. She had all but forgotten her encounter with Nintaka, the perentie, better known as a goanna, though there were other less fearsome animals along the way. Once a frilled lizard thinking it had to defend itself, its mouth wide open its neck extended in its characteristic striking "umbrella" had nearly frightened the life out of her but she had managed to swallow down a cry. Kangaroos were more friendly. They stood up on their powerful hind legs staring at them with mild curious eyes; a pair of superb looking golden dingoes moved with complete confidence through their wild habitat, totally ignoring them.

"Plenty of those through the park," Ross told her. "Generally they're pure bred. They hunt alone or maybe two together. You don't see them that often in groups."

"So what do they feed on?" Samantha, like every other Australian had heard the terrible, tragic story of Lindy Chamberlain's baby being taken by a dingo near Uluru.

"Small animals," he told her. "Birds, reptiles. Its not our native species we have to worry about, it's introduced species like the buffalo. They roam wild in the Territory particularly in the region of the Adelaide and Alligator rivers where they do great damage."

"Like what?"

"They wallow in the billabongs turning them into mud pools. They trample the vegetation. That's only the beginning."

"How did they come to be here in the first place?"

He checked a little so she could catch up with him. "They were introduced in the early 1800s from Timor to work the farms. When the settlements died out the bullocks were turned off to run wild. They flourished so much nearing the end of the 1800s they were hunted for their hides and horns. The market didn't decline until the mid '50s. The meat's dreadful by the way."

"But I thought the buffalo was a symbol of the Territory?"

He shrugged. "Well they've gone down in our folklore, I suppose, like the introduced camels in the Red Centre, but regardless both are large-scale destroyers of our fragile environment. Buffalo really are bulls in a china shop. Make no mistake. It isn't just the wallowing and trampling. They eat out the protein grasses our native herbivores depend on. Even the birds are affected by their presence. Don't start me on buffalo. As a cattleman I'm all for culling. They spread bovine disease. That alone threatens our beef industry. Feral pigs create similar problems. We have brumbies on North Star but they're a more limited problem."

"What about man?" she asked quietly. "The mines must have a big effect on the sensitive environment."

"Whatever *I* think," he said, "the fact is the mines are *there*. Ranger, Jabiluka, Jabiru, Koongarra. All we can do is work to minimize the adverse ecological *and* social impact."

"You feel very strongly about it."

"Of course I do. Don't you? This is one of the last remaining great wilderness areas in the world. This is my *home*."

"Well you're a very fortunate man." Her breath was a little laboured.

He stopped quickly and stared down at her. She was fit and she was strong but she *was* a young woman. "This has been a bit too much for you," he said, carrying on his inspection.

"Oh, I'm a bit puffed, that's all. I've been loving it."

His tone combined concern and anger directed against himself. "It's my damned fault," he frowned.

She struggled to stand perfectly upright, shoulders squared. "Ross, relax. I can puff once in a while, can't I? I'm perfectly all right."

"Well we're within spitting distance." He grunted and reached up to hold a low branch away from her head.

"I never knew you were such a fuss pot," she muttered, realising he was genuinely anxious about her.

"I have to blame *you* for that," he returned acidly.

For answer because she was getting to know his ways, she linked her arm companionably through his. "I think you must definitely like me."

He was faintly smiling. "You have heard the saying, she grew on me?"

"Well we do have a lot in common, don't you think?"

"Like what?"

She smiled at him sweetly, her velvet eyes glowing. "Both of us love a swim. What else?"

The sound of the waterfall grew louder. Moments later they were converging on a beautiful stretch of water the milky green of an opal.

Samantha pulled off her straw hat and began to fan herself with the wide brim. "This must be the Garden of Eden," she said with conviction.

"Not an apple tree in sight." Not that he needed any tempting.

"I think that biblical apple tree was more likely to have been a fig tree," she mused. "Look, plums, wild plums," she said excitedly, pointing to a clump of dark purple fruit. "Wild pear as well. I've never seen such a beautiful peaceful spot in my whole life."

He walked across the sand. "There are many like this in the region. Much more spectacular falls like Jim Jim which can only be viewed from a helicopter in the Wet."

"Thank you so much for bringing me." She gazed across table topped rocky outcrops where water swirled and eddied in a series of small crystal clear pools to the deeply furrowed cliff face of the escarpment. It glowed a bright orange in the sunlight with stria of white, yellow and black ochres. Foaming white waters cascaded across the summit and tumbled into the cool palm fringed lagoon below. "I consider it a real privilege to see this. I couldn't possibly have found it on my own."

The peace and the quiet of the place was remarkable; apart from the song of the falling waters and the clear, far carrying call of the birds.

"So, you want a swim?" He glanced at her expressive face, aware the heat had got to her. Despite that, her joyful responses were giving him immense pleasure. City girl she might be but she had a natural deep feeling for this ancient land. "Do you need to change?"

She shook her head. "I've come prepared. Where can we leave our packs?"

"Over there." He pointed to the widest section of sand, scattered with boulders so polished they glittered in the sun.

"Lovely!" Her heart beat speeded up. This was too fabulous to believe in. To be here in this paradise with *him*. Quite alone. She was light-headed with the excitement of it.

A minute more, she saw the long muscles of his sleek darkly tanned back. The narrowed waist. His jeans came away and she saw his strong straight legs, then the taut low line of his swimming briefs. She was half hypnotised by his male beauty. He was a beautiful sexy man. She coloured and felt something like static electricity pass through her body.

"Well?" He glanced back at her with an arched brow.

Her blush deepened, her heart racing as it did whenever he appeared. "I won't tell you," she said. "You're vain enough already."

"Now *that's* funny."

"You must know what you look like."

"Men don't spend their time staring into mirrors."

"Some men do. I know a guy who can't pass a mirror without checking himself out."

"God!" he said with droll disdain.

"So, let me get undressed." Suddenly overcome by shyness she waved him away.

He rolled his aqua eyes heavenwards. "I've already seen you in a bikini that wasn't a bit less revealing than necessary. I've seen your bra top through your shirt."

"This is a more cover-up version," she said, beginning to un-button her shirt. "You're not going to spring any crocs on me, are you? Because I'll freak out."

"You and me both!" He flicked a derisive smile at her and started to move off. "Don't keep me waiting."

Swiftly she started peeling off her cotton jeans. She couldn't be that close to him. Not all day, without something happening.

They waded into the water that quickly became deep underfoot. It was surprisingly cold considering the heat of the sun was full on it. Samantha sucked in her breath and began splashing water over her face and head so it began streaming water.

"Oh this is what I wanted!" she explained, turning her face up to the golden dazzling sun. "I'm going to swim across to the waterfall, okay?"

"Go for it!"

They both dived together, stroking strongly. It was a mar-vellous, exhilarating sensation being in the water after the long, hot trek. They swam together towards the falls that up close pounded rather than tumbled into the lagoon. Then they were right inside it, treading water. Samantha laughed with sheer bliss, reaching up to cup the sparkling water in her hands.

"Wonderful!" she shouted from the depths of her exalted state. She felt the energy of the cascading waters crackling deep inside her.

"You can say that again!" He was savouring this just as much as she was, his pleasure in their swim increased many times over by having her with him.

For almost an hour, they sported like a couple of dolphins,

gliding through the opal waters, lying on their backs so they could look up at the waterfall. The beneficial effect of the water was acting like a powerful therapy on Samantha's tired limbs. She felt reinvigorated, engulfed in physical and mental pleasure. She had the most wonderful of companions. So in harmony with her surroundings, she began to sing, a lovely old ballad she had learned long ago with the school choir, her voice soaring, pure and true.

He applauded thinking her voice had reached his heart, chasing away all the shadows, lighting up the darkest place in his soul. He couldn't remember when he had had such pleasure in a song, the lilting voice. Even the birds had joined in the chorus.

The song over she was calling to him. "Fancy having *this* in your backyard!" She threw up her arms, staring up at the illuminated cliff face.

The sky was cloudless; the deepest blue. They might have been alone in the garden of Eden complete with waterfall and deep lagoon.

Finally because they were hungry, they made for the shore, the sandy beach a pristine gold carpeted here and there with some kind of aquatic plant with frilly little yellow flowers in bloom.

Samantha pulled the pins from her hair, shook it out, then combed it away from her face with her fingers.

"You've had enough sun, you know," he warned, his muscles rippling as he ran a towel briefly over his body.

She replied with a languorous wave of her hand. "I'm wearing sunblock."

His slanted over her. "No arguments. Sunblock is not enough. We'll eat over there in the shade."

"Okay, boss." She'd brought with her a length of gauze, bright purple printed with huge white hibiscus which she tied sarong like around her waist. It wasn't much of a cover-up, but it would have to do.

"Feeling a bit better?" he asked. He had pulled on his jeans but left his darkly tanned torso bare.

"I feel great," she said, a little huskily, suspended between exhilaration and trepidation in equal measure. They couldn't have been more alone. She dropped her eyes to his backpack. "What have you got there?"

"Fruit," he clipped off, partly because he, too, was on a fine knife's edge. "Apples, bananas, some sandwiches Joe made for us wrapped in a cold pack. Couple of cokes, likewise. A packet of biscuits and a slab of chocolate in with the sandwiches."

"A feast in other words." Her pulses were beating like moths around a light. They were moving towards something momentous. She couldn't step back from it. She kept her eyes down, hoping her lashes veiled the sexual excitement that throbbed through her in waves.

A long swathe of her drying hair fell across her face. Pure copper. Her cheeks had the colour of peaches. Her mouth looked luscious. Had she looked up at that moment she would have seen him openly desirous. The driving need to make love to her had grown into an obsession, but from long habit Ross retained some control. He opened out the packed sandwiches, then pushed them towards her along with a crisp, red apple.

"I think I'll start on the apple first," she said, unaware the upward sweep of her glance was burning through all his defences. She bit into the crisp flesh with her small perfect teeth.

"Delicious!"

The shocking thing was the *force* of his need for her. The muscles of his arms were quivering with emotion. A trickle of apple juice dribbled down her chin and she brushed her creamy skin with the back of her hand.

That set him off. He moved as swiftly and powerfully as a big cat, reaching for her, one hand at the back of her head, the other grasping her around the waist. "You *know* this has been coming. Eve with the apple."

Her heart shook at the expression in his eyes. Their colour was a shock of pleasure every time she looked into them. She had no thought of protest even if she could have induced him to release her. She had *fantasised* about this. Now it was actually happening.

"My God, look at you," he groaned, her hair on fire in the dappled sunlight. "You're as beautiful as an angel."

Playing the angel was totally beyond her. "I'm a *woman* Ross. I don't want to be an angel." Angels didn't have desire moving in a rippling motion right through their body. Angels were chaste, far removed from earthly passions. She stared up at him, letting him draw her more fully into his arms. Her body was trembling, locked in a spasm of excitement as he gathered her in.

She couldn't speak. Instead she buried her face against his neck, aware of the wonderful male scent of him, the warmth of his skin, as she gently gripped his lean hips.

"Show your face to me." He nudged up her chin, with his thumb beneath, desperate to find her mouth; feel her lips give under the weight of his. Above all he wanted her to *feel* as he did.

His heart seemed to slip from behind his rib cage. He bent over her as she clung to him, kissing her for a long time, tasting, tongueing, exploring. That lovely soft, full mouth. Two minutes, three, four? Who was counting? It was ravishing beyond belief, mouth upon mouth, breath on breath. It was a form of expression that gave him heart-stopping pleasure yet soon it wasn't enough. It seemed to him they mated perfectly as though they had prior knowledge of each other. How was that possible? There wasn't the slightest brush of awkwardness, but instant magic as though their bodies and perhaps their souls were familiars in perfect accord.

Soon he drew back to stare at her, asking what he desperately wanted to know. "How far can I go, Samantha?" There was a hint of desperation in his voice. His hands stroked and slid across her skin hungrily, though he was still walking a tight rope. God only knew if he could regain full control. Maybe he would have to retreat to the tingling waters of the lagoon.

Samantha was shaking so much she couldn't get a word out. Her hair had tumbled to frame her impassioned face. She wasn't a virgin. Her first taste of sex at seventeen had been no wild adventure, just an odd disappointment with a boy she had known all her life. A nice boy who thought she had been as transported as himself.

"What if I never see you again after we leave this place?" she asked with a hint of melancholy.

"Maybe I won't let you go." His hands clenched on her shoulders. "I'll lock you up in the homestead. I'll never let you go back to the city."

"I must know what it is you want of me?"

"Your trust," he said ardently. "We can learn together." Powerless not to, he disengaged her bra top, hearing the catch snap with a faint twang. Her small perfect breasts were revealed. Creamy roses with a wine-red centre.

He lowered his head to her, his heart pounding so hard he might have had a raging beast caged inside of him.

Samantha bit so hard into her bottom lip she almost drew blood, arching her back as he took her budded nipple into his mouth. Ripple after ripple of sensation was rushing into her groin. She could have wept with the force of it. "Be gentle, Ross," she begged, excitement worryingly swamping her.

"Is it against the rules for me to suckle your breasts?" Shivers of pleasure were running over his whole body. He might have been some love-starved fool wanting more and more of her. He needed to explore her beautiful woman's body, her naked, flesh, her secret places. He was almost beyond thinking now. There was nothing but *sensation*.

"How can I say no to you," she muttered, turning her head this way and that, her eyes tightly closed so she could shut in the ecstasy of his caresses. "But then you know that."

He groaned harshly, lifting his head. "I would never take a defenceless woman against her will. I would never hurt you, Samantha. I speak of *trust*."

She opened her eyes then to discover a stricken look on his taut handsome face. "Trust there is, but you don't *love* me."

So why was this the greatest rapture he had ever known? "How can I love you when you won't let me?" he accused her.

"But I love *you!*" The words were ripped from her like a rending of flesh. Once said, would she live to regret them?

His face took on a daunting expression. "You don't mean that," he said flatly as though she'd been making a joke instead of declaring her heart.

Something painful heaved in her chest. "Does my loving you make you feel trapped?"

His gaze was turbulent. "If you made a commitment to me I'd *never* let you go. I don't know if you fully realise that."

"You're worried I might *want* to go?" she asked incredulously.

His eyes brooded on her highly charged face. "Why wouldn't I worry," he countered in a sombre voice. "This could all be an adventure for you. Great for a time but could you possibly settle into my kind of life?"

"Some things you can't entirely know, Ross. Life itself is a gamble."

"As far as marriage is concerned, no gamble," he told her bluntly. "Marriage *is* for life."

"So you're thinking more of an affair?" she asked emotionally, aching at that brooding expression.

"Does what we're doing mean so little to you?" he demanded. "I want you so much I just could damn myself forever. Ah, what's the use!" He hauled her to him, crushing her soft breasts against the hard muscled wall of his chest, revelling in the physical contact. A man would do anything for this.

"Don't turn against me," she begged.

"I think that's impossible," he said in a near despairing voice. He made one last effort to keep control, something inside of him continuing to fight her woman magic. "Is it a safe time for you or could I make you pregnant?" He stared down at her, eyes intent.

He could make me pregnant any time she thought wildly. She *ached* to one day give him a child. Children. Children who would all have his startlingly beautiful eyes. "It's a safe time," she flushed. Was any time completely safe? But the clamouring that beset her were too powerful to be denied. She threw up her glowing head, meeting his steady, questioning gaze. "I'm in love with you, Ross Sunderland, and no other man will do."

His emotions overflowed. "Say it again," he ordered, holding her captive for a moment before laying her on the rug. Her beauty filled his eyes. He looked at the tantalising triangle of blue lycra, all that was left to cover her naked body from his gaze.

"Dare I?" she whispered, transfixed by his expression which seemed to her to be beyond desire.

For answer he began to kiss her, his upper body curved over her, listening to her little moans as he moved lower and lower, the tip of his tongue savouring the silky texture of her skin.

"You're so beautiful," he whispered reverently and lifted her so he could remove the last remnant of clothing that separated her from his loving mouth and his hands.

After hours of driving around in search of potential sites David might want to capture, then more hours filming under a sapphire-blue sky, suddenly they came across some remarkably shaped rocky outcrops too low to be called hills. The surrounding savannah was covered in waving waist high dark golden grasses and beyond that a pocket of luxuriant tropical vegetation, an irresistible oasis.

"We can take a rest here," Joe said, looking across at David. They had taken it in turns to do the driving. Now Joe was at the wheel.

"A cup of tea would go down well," David smiled, each man easy in the other's company.

It was the bloke in the back who set off the alarm bells in the highly perceptive Joe. Something's wrong with him, Joe thought, listening to the warning voices in his head. Made a big deal out of the least little thing. Jealous of Ross, of course.

Wanted the young woman, Samantha. Take a lot more than that fella could offer to win such a woman.

He found a parking spot in the shadow of a crouching sand-stone monument and cut the engine. "I'll get the billy going," he said.

"Thanks, Joe," David said gratefully. "I can't give you high enough marks for looking after us."

"Long as you're happy," Joe showed his dazzling white teeth in a smile.

"How are *you* holding up, Isabelle?" David opened the rear door and helped her out, while Matt exited the other door in a somewhat stony silence, wandering off.

"Let's say I'm fine and hope to be for many, many years," she answered lightly, not daring to raise her head to him. The very last thing she had been expecting after the terrible trauma of Blair's death was to find another man—and *such* a man! The look of him, the sound of him, his laughter and the warmth of his deep voice—his kindness and his gentlemanly gestures. All this she found powerfully attractive. She might have *dreamed* him up so intense were her feelings. When he was driving she had sat up front beside him, torn between a kind of euphoria and despair that she could feel this way. There was a price to be paid for forbidden longings. The improbable had happened, she thought with fatalistic acceptance. She had fallen headlong in love with a man who was almost a stranger. But how could he be a *stranger,* when he seemed to know things about her she wouldn't even admit to herself.

A faint melancholy descended on her which David remarked with a clutch of the heart. He could sense she was upset about something and he found himself wanting to rock her tenderly in his arms. The rumours had been utterly wrong. This beautiful young woman was in mourning. She wouldn't thank him for any action on his part that could be interpreted as intimate. Intimacy couldn't happen even if she had such a dangerous fascination for him. At such a turning point in her life she needed her own space.

Sheltered by the sandstone outliers that surrounded it was a chain of small pools of an entrancing smoky blue that in the Wet became one large deep billabong. Now while it awaited the full onset of the rains the fresh water billabong had dried out to four shallow waterholes some distance apart. Rocky ledges formed a natural amphitheatre around the banks, the sandstone studded with chips of quartz that sparkled like semi precious gemstones in the sun.

Such a lovely place to rest! The ubiquitous pandanus lent a wonderfully cool feeling to the site. Many of the trees had sent down prop roots deep into the water. Others fanned their picturesque spikes over the ancient stone benches softening the contours of the weathered rock. Elsewhere flowering grevilleas, hibiscus and delicate eucalypt flowers stood out brilliantly against the rich greens of the vegetation and the curious blue of the water that nevertheless was so clear it was easy to see the sandy bottom scattered with more chips of quartz.

Joe got the billy going in no time while Matt prowled restlessly around the area trampling bright displays of little pink and white storm flowers under his heavy boots. At intervals he stood staring off into the wilderness with a rather fierce expression on his face. What was he thinking? At one point David went over to speak to him. Isabelle sat quietly observing without appearing to, watching Matt's thin face break into a smile. He shook his head at something David had to say and Isabelle found herself reluctantly empathising with Matt's position. Clearly he was very much in love with Samantha, a feeling Samantha definitely did not share. She wondered how Samantha's trek with her brother was working out. Well she hoped. She thoroughly approved of Samantha.

In some strange way Matt reminded her of Blair. Blair had that same *tension* inside him, the fear of being a failure, of being passed over. Blair had been plagued by a manic jealousy which culminated in violence. She just hoped nothing would happen to mar their trip. Not that Matt stood a chance of asserting him-

self over Ross or David. That would be like comparing a cub
with two full grown lions. It was tenderhearted Samantha he
might threaten. He only had to get her alone.

Isabelle breathed a sigh, watching David return. He made
directly for where she sat on the stone ledge, making a sweep-
ing gesture with his arm.

"I could be here a year or more and never run out of sites,"
he said with the greatest satisfaction. "Everything is progress-
ing so well. I have high hopes for this series." He moved back
to sit beside this beautiful creature who would have made the
most common place surroundings seem like heaven. "Thank
you again for sitting *and* standing so patiently while I photographed you. It couldn't have been all that easy, especially not
in the humid heat though you always look as cool as a lily."

"Well thank you, David." She dipped her head. "But goodness I'm used to it. I was born here. I'm a Territorian."

"And it shows. You're so much at home here. Yet you left it
for the city. I can't imagine it was easy to replant you. Then
again you were embarking on a new life."

"Yes," she agreed quietly, knowing he was desperate not to
hurt her by saying the wrong thing. "At the beginning I settled
in well." Blair had not revealed his true nature until much later.
"It was a very social life. We were out pretty well every night
of the week." Hadn't Blair been hell bent on showing her off
like some trophy? "I wasn't used to that as you can imagine,
having spent my life on North Star. After a while I have to say
all the partying became wearisome. A lot of it was quite mean-
ingless. People can be very insincere. Then again I seemed to
antagonise my mother-in-law and because of her Blair's whole
family. I know Mrs. Hartmann had already picked the right girl
for Blair to marry."

"One no doubt she could manipulate and control," he answered rather grimly.

She looked at him in surprise. "It sounds like you've met
Mrs. Hartmann?"

He shook his tawny head. "I have to admit I've heard a lot about her."

"Then you've also heard a lot about me." She had to accept it.

He smoothed over this. "Listening to gossip isn't high on my list, Isabelle. I've told you that."

"Nevertheless I fear you've heard something. You've been so nice to me, David. Going out of your way to comfort me."

"I'd do anything to help you, Isabelle. When I first met you, you seemed to be just coping with the pain. Nowadays you appear stronger."

"I feel it," she said. "I was like someone frozen, but the sun has warmed me through." The sun and *you*. He was always calming her in his powerful benign golden presence. Somehow he had given her back a sense of her own identity. Not Blair Hartmann's abused wife. Isabelle Sunderland as she had once been.

His sense of urgency grew. Could she intuit his powerful desire to hold her close? Day after day it got harder not to take her in his arms. He had never with his passing lovers experienced such a rush of emotion.

For a moment Isabelle felt almost transparent under his topaz gaze. As if all the agony with Blair she had kept so secret, so hidden, might be there for him to see. Somewhere close a bird called. It seemed to be the only sound in this paradise. "I find myself very anxious to correct any false impressions, David," she said. "Your good opinion means a lot to me."

"Hello?" He couldn't help himself. He caught the point of her chin with his finger turning her beautiful poignant face towards him. "Don't you know you've got it."

Of their own accord tears glistened in her eyes. "I've already told you my marriage wasn't working out, David. At least the gossips were right about that."

"And you're blaming yourself?" Reluctantly he dropped his hand.

Her eyes were fixed but blurred. How much could she expose of herself? She felt such shame. Would he feel disgust?

"It seems to me I *am* to blame," she said sadly. "Small wonder Blair's mother hates me."

He stepped up his defence. "You had *nothing* to do with his death."

"I know that with my head." She touched a hand to her temple. "In my heart there's a lot of guilt. Blair turned out to be different from the man I thought I'd married. Sometimes I think he only married me to spite his mother."

He frowned at the absurdity of that. "Surely not. I've been told he was passionately in love with you."

"Not me," she said quietly. "Not the *real* me. I, in turn, was quite different from the woman Blair thought he had married. There was a lot of pain in our marriage. Especially towards the end."

"You sound like you felt *trapped?*" He studied her closely, trying to see through the layers and layers of defences she had set up to protect herself.

"I was trying to find a way out of it."

Suddenly she sounded greatly determined causing him to hesitate. This wasn't what he had thought. It was more in keeping with the general view. Her husband had adored her. She had denied him her love. *The Ice Queen* was the label that had been thrown around. Was it *possible?* For all her beauty and charm something about her sent the message not to reach out and touch her. "You never spoke to your father or Ross?" he asked.

His eyes rested on her like a warm golden glow. "The damnable sin of pride."

Pride and vanity. He had seen little evidence of it.

"I've shocked you." For a moment her very soul was naked.

"Hardly shocked, Isabelle," he said. Something far less certain and subtle. An inclination to question. Get to the bottom of it but he had no right. "Unhappy marriages aren't terribly unusual."

"You're doubting that I tried?"

Those appealing eyes couldn't have been more alluring. "I'm sure you did. Nevertheless you've been allowing your feelings of guilt to grow."

"Now why did I start on this?" she asked, a tremor in her voice.

He caught her hand and just barely stopped himself from carrying it to his mouth. "Obviously you need someone to talk to. I think you've learned to trust me."

"In a remarkably short time." Her voice was barely above a whisper.

"And what you might tell me you've never told another soul?"

She winced. "You make it sound like I have terrible secrets."

"*Do* you?" It was worse not knowing. He had to remember she had been abandoned by her mother as a child. That had dire consequences. A replay of the pattern? She had grown up in an all male household albeit a loving and protective one. Her husband, her lover, had failed her. She had failed him. How?

"I daresay all of us take some things to the grave." She looked up as a flight of pure white corellas landed in a stunted acacia covering the branches like so many large floppy flowers.

"I don't think you could have experienced anything *that* bad?"

Misery that only ended with Blair's death. Misery she found she couldn't possibly share. Not even with David. She had to hide the things Blair had done to her though they would stay with her forever. A normal person would consider her either a masochist or a coward. She was neither. Put simply, it was just she had been in such a state of shock, of denial, to cope with Blair when he turned on her.

David could see her withdrawal to a quiet place in her own soul.

"I have to deal with things by myself," she said, turning her head and looking into his eyes. "I have to start a new life. I *have* started. I'm much better being active. This trip is working its own magic. I'm glad I came. I'm honoured you wanted to put me in your photographs. I think I was a little more than the subtle human element, wasn't I?" She couldn't help but know he had used her as a *focus,* the element that drew the eye rather than a background figure.

"Ah, so you noticed!" His deep voice was self-mocking.

"You're a very beautiful woman, Isabelle. The camera loves you. Plus you have close ties with this landscape. In fact I'm mesmerised by the way you move about in it. The easy grace and the confidence. The way you *listen* for sounds. Sounds of danger, sounds of pleasure. When I asked for a certain pose today—not easy when you're not a professional model—your concentration was absolute. You worked with me to get the best shot possible. That means a lot. You even consented to wearing this outfit." He raised a fold of her skirt slightly so the sunlight shone through it making it shimmer. Desire closed in. He had to grapple with that like he had to grapple with a monster. "Not your usual safari gear," he commented lightly. He hadn't wanted that look, but something flowing and feminine which still blended with the wild environment. She had chosen wonderfully well. An ankle length skirt and a matching loose top that nevertheless clung to the contours of her body and showed the beautiful shape of her breasts. The material was semi transparent when the sun shone through it, the fascinating black, brown and burnt umber design on the sage green fabric had aboriginal motifs which were outlined in dots of yellow. On her feet she wore ethnic type sandals with the thin straps wound around her elegant legs to mid calf. With her long centre parted raven hair tumbling down her back he couldn't have had a more stunning subject.

Isabelle's blood raced and her heart tingled. He had perfected a lightness and calmness when he was with her but she knew in her heart it was carefully cultivated. Perhaps he felt *exactly* as she did? "And less hot." She smiled. "But the sandals aren't good for tramping. Are you going to shoot more film today?"

"More of the sunset," he said, waving back at Joe who was signalling all was in readiness. "They're unbelievably brilliant up here in the Top End. There's something very exciting in the lighting. I'm awaiting my opportunity to capture a midnight thunderstorm."

She smiled at his enthusiasm. "You sound like you have an endless love for your work."

"Love is the poetry of the senses." He gazed down at her for a moment, before taking her by the hand and leading her the short distance over the sand to the waiting afternoon tea.

Maybe one day in the weeks ahead, as they grew closer, she would confide what troubled her and what had caused her to rebel so violently—and she *had,* for all her reticence—against the confines of her doomed marriage. Only then was he going to do what was in his heart.

CHAPTER EIGHT

GREAT flights of water birds, glossy ibises and pied heron passed to the east of them, boring into the swamps, that were ideal sanctuaries. They were out on a broad tributary of the Alligator river, misnamed by an early explorer who mistook the far more dangerous crocodiles for their less ferocious brothers. Samantha was brimming with bravado and it had to be confessed, tingling nerves as though one of these monsters could attack the launch. During the morning's trip up river she saw for the first time in her life, basking in the hot sun, the giant prehistoric reptiles that had outlived the dinosaurs. Their pale yellow mouths were open even though they were at rest, showing their fearsome teeth.

"That's to reduce the effect of the heat on their brain," Ross told her. "It's called thermo-regulating. It's how they retain a body temperature of around thirty, thirty-two degrees C."

He was talking quite nonchalantly, but he was avidly aware of her as she was of him. *Passion* hummed like a wire stretched taut between them. The rapture of the lovemaking they had shared at the waterfall was the powerful current that fused them together. It kept them awake at night, separated, each in their respective tent, as their bodies longed for release from the never ending pressure of sexual desire.

Now Ross steadied her by the shoulders as she shied back instinctively. "It's okay. We're quite safe."

"I'll have to take your word for it."

He just laughed. As a Territorian he had lived with the presence of crocodiles all his life. Indeed they inhabited his back yard, hidden away in the deep and mysterious lagoons on North Star. No hot and weary stockman out on muster would dream of plunging into one though a visitor in the early 1920s had and paid for it with his life. From time to time horses and even stray cattle had disappeared on the station and the blame was always laid at the jaws of a croc. Kangaroos with their small brains had never learned not to drink from the swamps, lagoons and rivers consequently they often fell prey.

He lifted one hand from her shoulder and pointed as a "big fella" well over twenty feet long began its muddy slide into the water.

"Oh my God!" She shuddered, staring at the huge muscular body with its distinctive gnarled skin. "It's *black* isn't it? I thought they were grey?"

"Grey, dark brown, close to black like that old-timer."

"I've never seen anything so frightening in my life. Imagine being taken by one. It would have to be worse than being taken by a shark."

"You can take your pick up here," he said laconically. "The crocs, the estuarine crocodiles, the salties have no predators outside man. They're feared by all creatures."

"Which doesn't come as a surprise." The crocodile she was watching and David at the front of the launch was filming had submerged. Only its yellow eyes and its high ridged nostrils were visible above the surface of the water like some reptilian submarine. "Easy to see how they sneak up on you." Samantha was experiencing both horror and fascination.

"They float, keeping just the right degree of buoyancy to remain hidden," Ross explained. "Among reeds, water lilies and their pads, any floating debris. Then they spring with astounding speed for so cumbersome an animal."

"And eat you on the spot?" She let out an involuntary moan, thinking of the cases she had read about in the newspapers.

"No. Crocs only eat about once a week. They drown their prey in the famous death roll, dismember them and store them away underwater to eat later."

"How gruesome."

"There's a black side to Nature," he said. "A dark side. Magnificent as the Park is, it has it. In the old days crocs were aggressively hunted for their skins. Handbags, shoes, luggage, whatever. These days they're protected though God knows there are enough of them. I'll all for a controlled cull. I think you'd find most experienced bushmen are."

"So where does the expression 'crying crocodile tears' come from? Do they actually cry?"

He lowered his head closer to her ear, relishing the fresh scent of her. God only knew when they could be alone again. It couldn't come soon enough so urgent was his need. "Only when they've been out of the water for a long time, like in the Dry. At night in the relative cool they race overland from one dried out pool to find another with more water. As a sight, it's extraordinary. They cover the ground with incredible speed, holding those log like bodies up high on their short stumpy legs. Their 'tears' are only a fluid produced by the glands to protect and lubricate the eye. They're not emotional hence the saying. It's the breeding season right now until about April."

"But we're going on land. Surely that's a huge hazard?"

"Don't worry. We'll pick the right spot and the right time. During the breeding season the crocs just like the perentie you encountered become quite aggressive. Dominant males kill other males or badly injure them. The females attack one another as well. Dads are known to eat the eggs or their hatchlings if they can get to them but the female guards her nest well. The much bigger males back down just as a big man can be intimidated by his little wife."

She gave a soft, breathy laugh. "How extraordinary! Praise be there weren't any crocs in our beautiful lagoon. We could have been death rolled."

His voice was dry. "I hate to tell you this, my beautiful Samantha, but saltwater crocs can and do live in fresh water."

"You're joking!" She spun around to face him, meeting his gleaming, teasing eyes.

"Never! It's a myth saltwater crocs are only at home in salt water. There have been many many sightings in fresh water. A lone croc will stake out a lagoon or a billabong for himself at the end of the wet season especially if it has a good supply of barramundi and God help any young male croc who tries to come into the marked territory."

"You're not telling me there could have been a croc at the falls?"

"Would I put the woman I'm crazy about in danger?" He slid his hands around her waist, drawing her back against him.

"Ross…" she murmured.

"It's like a fever isn't it?" he said, his chin resting on her hair. "I want you so badly I'd take on six crocs. I have to find a time we can be together, even if it's only to kiss you. But first we have to lose your boyfriend," he tacked on sardonically.

"It'll be a challenge!" Her eyes moved to the front of the boat. Everyone else was preoccupied, but Matt, was staring their way, his expression masked by the deep brim of his hat.

A trickle like an icicle slid down Samantha's back. This was getting to be ridiculous. Anyone would think Matt was a rejected long time lover instead of a friend she had shared casual outings with. Why hadn't she taken note of this infatuation sooner? Like a blind fool she had drifted thoughtlessly into the path of trouble. She had no wish to hurt him.

Ross, his back to the other man, missed Matt's concentrated stare entirely. It might have made him call something challenging back. Samantha was all for avoiding confrontations.

In the heat of midafternoon, when the crocodiles indulged their love of a snooze on the banks, the skipper of their charter boat, a wiry little man nicknamed "Goldy" because he had once

mined a fair sized nugget on the Queensland goldfields, pulled
alongside a timber jetty that looked like it would collapse as
soon as the next strong breeze hit it. Ross sprang out of the boat
with the rope to tie the motor launch up. Large patches of
spiked rushes grew around the bleached grey-white of the
splayed jetty legs, the golden tips waving with the motion of
the wavelets caused by the wake of the boat.

"All right, ladies and gentleman," Goldy announced, standing on the salt stained deck, feet apart, hands behind his back.
"I'll be here, drinkin' until around five-thirty at which time I'd
like to depart. Which reminds me, Rossie, darlin'. Didn't yah
tell me you'd have a bottle of whiskey for me next time you
saw me?"

"A promise is a promise, Goldy," Ross called from the jetty.
"I'll give it to you before we leave. No use looking for it either."

"Spoil sport!" Goldy grinned. "Watch where yah put your
feet now. See yah all later."

The picturesque pandanus leaned at extraordinary angles the
cause of which was the prevailing winds. They stood out black
in silhouette against the dazzle of light from the sun and the
white sandy beach which was ringed heavily with dark green
vegetation overhung by the lacy canopy of trees.

On their trek through the trees the women were flanked by
Ross and David, while Joe and Matt brought up the rear. Joe's
trained eyes moved everywhere. Along the ground and through
the foliage checking out the possible presence of snakes not that
they weren't more frightened of humans than humans were of
them. But here beside the river, the vegetation was more mark-
edly tropical. The eucalypts that were dominant in the woodland
gave way to cottonwoods and myrtles that soared a hundred feet
and more. Great buttress roots impeded their progress, the whole
area covered with lichen, mosses, ferns and vines.

They had travelled some distance before they came on a welcome clearing where great banyan trees whose massive bull

could withstand the fiercest monsoon spread their giant arms over a wide area offering shade and a good camp site.

Samantha gave a little exclamation of pleasure. "Aren't they magnificent?"

"According to my people, the Gunwinggu, our 'mother' Waramurungundji created the banyan tree at the very beginning of Creation." Joe supporting himself with a stout branch spoke up. "Our legendary ancestors came from across the sea by canoe from maybe the direction of Indonesia," Joe continued, knowing how eagerly this young white woman received and soaked up the legends and oral traditions of his tribe.

"Hasn't science arrived at similar conclusions," David asked.

Joe grunted wryly. "When Moses led his people out of Egypt, *my* people had been occupying this region of the Alligator Rivers for more than twenty thousand continuous years. We are the *first* Australians."

"No argument there, Joe." Ross turned his head over his shoulder. "Tell Samantha about the adventures of Waramurungundji's husband."

"How I like the way you roll that off your tongue." Samantha was impressed. Some aboriginal names were very difficult. "She had a husband?"

"Wuragag." Joe nodded. "But she wasn't his only wife. He had many wives, wicked old man. Many adventures. At the end of his earthly life he was turned into a high rocky hill which you will see sometime soon. It dominates the plains north of Oenpelli. A lot of white people call it Tor Rock. We call it Wuragag. There's a smaller rock beside it that's his favourite young wife, Goringal."

"And the Oenpelli region is where we'll find much of your great aboriginal artistic heritage, Joe?" Samantha asked.

"Our *major* heritage," Joe answered. "Arnhem Land is very rich in our culture. It houses outstanding rock galleries of great antiquity."

"And we have you to interpret them for us, Joe," Samantha smiled back at him, receiving a beaming acknowledgment in return.

Many hundreds of feet of film had already been shot and packed up ready for processing in Darwin. Almost as many more shots on the digital camera had been printed off allowing them all to see work in progress; David's powerful and often moving evocations of a unique region. The rain forests, wetlands and woodlands, its remarkable flora and fauna, the magnificent bird life, the innumerable species of water birds alighting on lily covered lagoons, the brilliantly coloured parrots and parakeets with their long green and blue tail feathers, the honey eaters, the colourful Gouldian finches, the blue winged kookaburras and the sacred kingfishers, as well as the birds of prey, the eagles, falcons and the osprey.

Today was the crocodile's turn. Ross carried the rifle as a necessary precaution, Joe had a lethal looking hunting knife thrust through his belt. Even Isabelle in safari gear like Samantha had some sort of knife in a sheaf strapped to the tan leather belt around her waist Samantha noted without surprise. Isabelle who was as elegant as any top fashion model was equally at home in this wild bush setting. But then she had been born to it.

"So what's the plan? Where are we going?" Samantha asked, her face vivid with excitement.

Ross shook his head gently. "Not *you*, Samantha. Not this time."

She came back to earth with a great thud. "What do you mean? Isabelle's going."

"Belle *has* offered to stay." Ross turned his head briefly to where Isabelle was passing some piece of equipment to David. "She's made countless forays into the bush in the past. Dad and often Joe used to take us from when we were children. She's had a lifetime of experience. You haven't."

"So I'm disqualified on that count?" She looked at him, temper ignited by deep disappointment.

"Don't take it like that." He gave her the sudden smile that so illuminated his face. "The very last thing I want is to put you in any danger. It's obvious the crocs freak you out and David wants to film their nests."

"He must be mad," she said, fuming at being excluded. "I might have a word with him."

Ross shook his head. "It would do no good. We've discussed it. Neither of us wants to risk taking you. You're very precious."

"Precious be damned!" She stared up at him, more affected than she should have been. "You're fobbing me off. You never wanted me here in the first place."

"Ah, Sam," he groaned.

"Don't 'Sam' me," she said, flushed and hurt.

"It *is* your name. I don't think I've heard David call you Samantha once."

"David's my *brother*. You've had this whole thing planned. You knew on the boat, yet you never told me."

"Hang on," he said firmly. "I should have known you'd have quite a temper." Her hair in fact was a fiery corona in the sunlight. "You've been in on just about everything. This particular trip has been ruled out for a very good reason. For one thing we'll be moving with the utmost caution. Crocs take great exception to anyone approaching the nest. A goanna frightened the living daylights out of you. I can't risk your letting out a scream if you spotted a python, a feral pig or even another perentie. There are plenty of them about. You just don't see them for much of the time. It would be risky to even make a peep where we're going."

"You're making out I'm an absolute idiot."

She went from fire to ice very quickly. "No such thing. All I'm saying is, you're inexperienced in the bush especially in this kind of situation. Think about it, Samantha."

"But I *want* to go," she insisted, not yet able to control her disappointment.

"You're not going and that's the end of it," he said firmly. "I'm sorry. I'll make it up to you. If it's any comfort, we won't be gone long. You can be sure of that. David will have to work very quickly in a dangerous situation but he's well used to that."

She blinked back hot tears, embarrassed they were there. "And just what am I supposed to do while the rest of you have gone adventuring? Sit under the banyan tree and sing calypso songs."

"Why not?" he asked with humour. "I've heard you sing. In fact I'll never forget it. You have the sweetest voice."

"I'll stay right back." She tried a last time, fixing her eyes on his face.

"*No*. You're too used to getting your own way. This one expedition has been judged too dangerous. Please don't take it personally."

It was hard to realise this was the man she *loved!* "Well I *am* taking it personally," she announced, the knot in her stomach working its way up into her throat. "You're such a hero you could carry me on your shoulders."

He studied her with his startling eyes. "You'll have to get your weight down by at least twenty kilos."

She was shocked into incoherence. "Whh-aa-t?"

A smile curved his lips. "A joke, *Samantha*."

"Well it hasn't cheered me up." Her shoulders slumped. "All right go off and leave me."

"Don't sulk. I only want the best for you."

"Now isn't that fine and dandy. For your information I am not sulking. I am hurt and disappointed. Some days, Ross Sunderland, you remind me of a really big bully."

"When I'm trying to look after you? Have a heart!"

Isabelle who had been watching this mild confrontation and knowing what it was all about, crossed the clearing to join them. "You're disappointed, Sam?"

Samantha tried to rally but found she couldn't. "Well I'd planned on coming, Belle."

Isabelle touched her hand consolingly. "I've been on these trips before. They can get scary, I promise you. No one is doubting you're game for anything but something might cross our path to give you a fright. No one could blame you if you cried out."

"*You* wouldn't react?" Samantha asked, trying to see it through Isabelle's eyes.

Ross cut her short. "No she *wouldn't* Samantha. Accept that."

"Anyway I'm staying with you." Isabelle made the swift decision.

Matt who had been eavesdropping all the while saw his golden opportunity. Oh my, oh my, to get Sam on her own! Wasn't this what he'd been waiting for? He straightened his shoulders, put a winning smile on his face and wandered up to join them. "Did I hear you offer to stay with Sam, Isabelle?" he asked, refinding his old charm.

"Really I'll be quite all right on my own," Samantha protested, knowing Isabelle was only being kind. She really wanted to go.

"You don't have to be," Matt was the picture of supportiveness. "David doesn't need me right now I'm relieved to say, so I'm free to keep you company."

A slight frown crossed Ross's face. "That's nice of you, Matt, but Belle doesn't mind."

To pique him Samantha succeeded in hiding her true feelings. "I don't want Isabelle to miss out on account of me," she said.

"I'm not *that* keen to go, Sam," Isabelle assured her, wary of the way Matt could change his persona in the blink of an eye. Hadn't she seen it all before?

"What's the problem?" Matt turned up his palms, looking innocently around the group. "Sam and I have shared many a pleasant hour. We're used to being together. We can settle back and relax while the rest of you go in search of where the crocodile makes his nest. As far as I'm concerned it's healthier here."

"So that's settled," Samantha said, making a great effort to appear bright and accepting and actually achieving that end. "Matt and I will remain here until you get back."

David who had finished assembling his equipment came their way. "I know it's not what you want, Sam, but I'd feel much happier if you stayed in camp. Isabelle has agreed to keep you company."

"There's been a change of plan," Samantha gave him an easy smile. "Belle's going. I know she wants to. Matt has kindly offered to stay with me."

Something flickered in David's golden eyes. "Who decided this?"

"*I* did," Samantha lied smoothly before Ross was allowed to break. "You'll only be gone an hour or two. Matt and I can do our own exploring."

"I'd rather you didn't," Ross clipped off.

"It would be best, Samantha," Isabelle offered, more gently.

"We'll be quite happy here," Matt intervened, his expression suggesting he thoroughly agreed with Ross and Isabelle. "A couple of hours will pass in no time at all."

"Better them than us," Matt said. The hunting party had long gone and they had finished exploring their immediate environment without venturing too far. "Crocodiles are too gruesome for words."

"I just hope one of them doesn't decide to go walkabout while their mates are asleep," Samantha said, moving over to the shade of a mighty banyan. It had a great central section of some hundred of trunks and scores of small trunks slender as saplings ringing the perimeter of the trees' branches where the birds had dropped the seeds and the sprouting seeds had taken root.

"Isn't this a fantastic tree," she said, not much liking being stuck with Matt but determined to make the best of it. These days he seemed to be two people. The old Matt she thought she knew and the *other* Matt, a far less pleasant character.

Matt looked up just as the fig like fruit of the banyan dropped to the ground. "Indian, aren't they? I remember a photograph Dave took of one in Sri Lanka. I wouldn't worry too much about crocs going walkabout around here. At least Macho Man knows what he's about. He's bound to have picked the right time and the place to find a nest or two." Matt lowered himself to the sand beside her, thrilled they were on their own at last with no one to disturb them. "I can't imagine why you wanted to go, Sam or Isabelle for that matter although Dave's the big attraction, not the crocs. For some reason she's trying to get her hooks into him."

"And it only took you a half a second to figure it out?" she said in a voice that should have warned him.

"Pretty much." He chewed on the side of his thumb. "I saw how she was with him that first night at the showing. People pressing in on all sides wanting to talk to him but she managed to find his ear."

"I'm not surprised. Isabelle is a very beautiful woman. Men tend to seek out beautiful women. Bachelor that he is, my brother is very susceptible to beauty."

"Well he's bending double to please her." Matt grunted, not bothering to hide his disapproval.

"Why don't you like her, Matt? You're so ready to condemn her when she's so charming and understanding."

"She has a *history,* Sam, remember?" He unsheafed his expensive sunglasses and shoved them on his nose. "Consider the events of her life. The lead up—the broken home. Mother going off. Inevitably that sort of thing has its effect. Hence, the bad marriage. You know the old saying there's no smoke without fire. I don't want to bring this up again, but I think you should be concerned. I know how much you love Dave. You wouldn't want to see him hooked by a woman like that. Women who chew a man up and spit him out."

"That, actually, is your very jaundiced opinion. Are you sure you're not referring to something in *your* past?"

"My past was quite ordinary," he lied. His parents had been

too busy battling each other to bother about him. But he had survived them both.

"Anyway, David can look after himself better than anyone I know," Samantha said, intensely irritated by this line of talk.

Matt gave a sceptical shrug. "You said yourself Dave is highly susceptible to beauty. I have to admit she's a looker if you like the type. I see her as a cold shallow person, untouchable, no real feeling or emotion there, yet she's a manipulator of men. Dave's a strong guy, but you should have seen him the day they spent together. The time and trouble he went to, to photograph her. Forget the scenery, it was Isabelle he focused on."

"And it will come out wonderfully," Samantha said loyally. "For the record, and I happen to have met quite a few people in my life plus the fact I'm supposed to be 'highly perceptive' according to one book review, I think Isabelle is simply beautiful. In every way."

"You don't know her." He gave a short bark of a laugh. "Or her brother. There's something about those two. They're heartbreakers. Believe me too many people were of the opinion Hartmann was a nice guy, willing to give her *everything* he loved her so much. It couldn't have been enough. Word is she told him she was going to leave him. I ask you! A couple of years of marriage and she wants out. Sunderland is the big he-man, the macho figure, the bloody cattle baron with a homestead much too big for ordinary people and jammed packed with stuff most people could never afford. Don't get too close to him, Sam. I feel it my duty to warn you. Like his sister I have him pegged for a callous breaker of hearts."

"Could it be you're jealous?" she asked bluntly, not caring if he was offended. She wondered how far the party had gone. She could run after them.

"Jealous?" Matt repeated the word. "Hell it's more like being flayed alive seeing the two of you together. You'd be better off without someone like him in your life, Sam," he said turning to her urgently. "He'd make a bloody awful husband, arrogant bastard. I care so much about you can you blame me if I feel the greatest concern?"

"Don't do this, Matt," she said.

"I *have* to. These days I rarely get the opportunity to speak to you alone."

Her nerves grated. "It's never occurred to you I can handle my own life? That includes the men in it."

"*Most* men, Sam," he emphasised. "Not this guy. He's different."

"He is indeed."

He took it badly; the soft expression on her face. "I'm only trying to warn you as a friend, Sam. Please don't take it the wrong way."

"So what do you think could happen? Tell me?" she challenged, her warm, musical voice slightly harsh.

He looked back at her, eyes concealed, his thin face colouring up a little. "He's working on you like his sister is working on Dave. He's not married. Why not? He must be thirty or thereabouts? Perhaps he prefers affairs?"

"A lot of men do even when they're married." She said dryly. Her own father among them.

"That wouldn't be *my* way," he said and caught her fingers. She had beautiful hands. He could see one of those slender fingers wearing *his* ring. "You're so beautiful, Sam. I couldn't bear to lose you to someone like Sunderland."

She dragged her hand away, thinking she should get up and run. Why oh why had she acted as if she were quite relaxed about staying with Matt? Because she had wanted to flout Ross. She had wanted to let him know he couldn't control her. "Matt, knowing me as long as you have," she asked with exaggerated patience, "have I *ever* given you reason to believe we could become something more than friends?"

"A man can catch a star, Samantha," he said. "Hold it in his hand. You're not serious about anyone. I've seen them come and go. At least not serious until you had the misfortune to run into Sunderland. You could have any guy you wanted. They were all standing in line but you chose to come out with *me*. You know why?"

"No, Matt, I don't," she lamented.

"It's because you know you can *trust* me." He whipped off his glasses and stared into her eyes. "Can you really and truly say you *trust* Sunderland? He's a wild card. Just look into *his* eyes. Spooky eyes, I reckon. He's a dangerous guy. This trip is nearly over. Dave isn't going on to the Red Centre. He's concentrating on the Top End. He has to be in Brunei early next month anyway."

"I know that. David does discuss his itinerary with me."

"Well then, you know the trip is nearly over. I know he wants to photograph the Arnhem Land escarpment and get to see all the rock art but he's more for evoking the moods of the land. He's already said when the Wet really gets underway he wants to come back and do a lot of filming from a helicopter. Much of the place, the wetlands, will be inundated and the major waterfalls will be inaccessible by land. Dave likes filming things in a completely different way."

Samantha glanced around the broad clearing not quite knowing what she was looking for, but taking stock. "I know my brother's work, Matt. I *sell it*. I've even sold yours."

"Of course you have," he said immediately. "No one better. You do a marvellous job of running the gallery. You must want to go back to it?"

"Anyone can sell, Matt," she pointed out.

"That's not quite true. Not all that many are as good with people as you are. That's a gift. *I* couldn't do it. I couldn't charm visitors to the gallery into buying."

"David's work sells itself, Matt. I think you're overestimating my powers of persuasion. I could find someone to take over from me. In fact I know someone who could make a change over a smooth transition. I actually want to *write*. Not just children's stories which I enjoy but mainstream fiction. At least I'd like to give it my best shot."

"Good for you!" Matt smiled at her delightedly, looking for a moment his old amiable self. "You need to stretch yourself to the limit. You need to travel. I can see the two of us wandering the world." His hazel eyes lit up. "I know you're attracted to Sunderland now. God knows he's a handsome devil, and he wants as much as he can get of you, but you'd be a plain fool to lay your emotions bare. He'll use you, then when you're gone, he'll pick up with someone else and begin all over again. One day he'll get around to marrying—some suitable girl from a rich pastoral family—someone who understands life on the land. That's the way it goes, isn't it? They marry their own. It won't be *you*, Sam. You couldn't survive the life. You'd wither and die. You're too bright and beautiful—you have too much to offer—to be stuck in the wilds with all your dreams trampled on. You can't have missed he's a domineering bastard."

That really stirred up her anger. "Well he's certainly the dominant male but *domineering*, no," she said forcefully. "I didn't stay back, Matt, to listen to your bitter criticisms of the Sunderlands. I think them unfounded."

"Lordy, Lordy me! Don't get angry. It's because you don't *want* to believe them, Sam."

She made one last attempt to turn him off his line of thinking. "Matt, can't we drop the subject or I might have to take a hike." Surely she could walk a little distance. She could take a stout stick like Joe or maybe pick up a rock for protection. There were plenty of them scattered about.

But Matt wasn't about to be deflected. He wanted to get it all off his chest. "God, weren't you humiliated when he told you to stay put like you were a child?" He sneered.

"This is what's called ear abuse, Matt," she said shortly. "Ross told us to stay put for a very good reason. Both of us are out of our depth in this kind of environment."

"There were nicer ways of saying it," Matt protested, suddenly seizing hold of her wrist.

"Matt, that hurts!" She jerked away, rubbing her skin.

"I could never hurt you," he said, shaking his head from side to side. "I love you. You're magic. I've wanted you ever since Dave introduced us. I've learned to be patient. I have photographs of you all over the walls of my flat."

"*Me?* You *can't* have."

Her lovely face registered not surprise and pleasure but utter dismay. "*Beautiful* photographs," he insisted, stung by the repudiation in her voice. "The thrilling part was you never even knew I was there."

A moan escaped her. "Matt, that's sick."

"Don't spoil anything, Sam." He stared at her with a peculiar gleam in the depths of his eyes. "How do you define *sick* anyway? How do you define love?"

She tried to push up but he pulled her back. "Matt, you're getting right out of line here," she said sharply. "You'd better reel yourself in. The last thing I want to do is tell David you're starting to harass me. I don't think he'd like that." She didn't like to think how Ross would handle it either.

Matt shut his eyes, his expression deeply offended. "Tell me what I have to do to convince you I love you. *Tell* me. I'll do anything."

"Right!" Samantha seized the moment and stood up. "Go jump in the river. It will cool you off."

"It's no joke, Samantha." He stood and took a few threatening steps towards her. "You're mine, Sam. Forever mine. He stole you."

"You're not trying to scare me, surely?" She stared at him, willing him to regain control.

"Be *nice*, Samantha," he begged, giving her the sweetest smile. "Otherwise I might hurt you. I wouldn't want to but your little jabs are coming close to my heart."

"You're losing it, Matt," she warned him. "If I were you, I'd get some professional advice."

"Would you now?" The attractive mask slid off. He came at her at a lunge, determined to knock some sense into her as his father had to do to bring his mother under control, but the little bitch turned on her heel and ran.

"Samantha!" he yelled. "What the hell! Come back."

She stumbled. Fell over a prop root and crashed to the sand.

He was on top of her, his skin paled to a curious grey patched with red. "Samantha what are you doing?"

"What are *you* doing, more like it!" she yelled. "Get off me. Have you gone quite mad?"

"Mad, yes." He struck her across the face, stealing her breath away. "He's had you, hasn't he?" He grasped her long hair, tugging it back painfully as he lifted her face to him. This wasn't working out at all like he expected. *Nothing* was.

Nightmare time Samantha thought, her heart quaking, her voice full of fury and outrage. "How *dare* you hit me. How *dare* you!"

Incredibly he began to mumble. "Oh I'm sorry, sorry. Forgive me, Sam. You made me so angry. It was your fault. You shouldn't do that. Just let me kiss you and make up." He forced his mouth down over her, his teeth grinding against hers, which were clenched tight against the invasion of his tongue. His fingers dug in to prise her jaws apart.

"Planning to rape me, Matt?" she gritted, struggling for all she was worth. She would never have believed Matt was so strong. "Try that and there's nowhere you can run."

He scarcely heard her, trying to fight his old demons. The black anger that wouldn't die. It was stirring within him, egging him on.

Take your medication and you'll live a normal life, Matt.

He had, with or without it. Until *now*.

The eyes staring back at her were empty. Samantha knew he couldn't get his will to obey him. Let someone come, she prayed, knowing no one was going to come. She had to brave this out. Get through by herself. She had to *fight*.

Silence was so thick and heavy around them their harsh breathing sounded almost inhuman. She feigned surrender, allowing her body to sink back into the sand. His demands were only going to increase.

I won't let this happen. I won't!

She'd have to hit him with something. A rock. A rock big enough to control him. They were all over the place. She spread-eagled her arms as if she were in ecstasy, her fingers searching…burrowing…while she sucked in air between his vile kisses.

Oh, let it stop!

She writhed further sideways pretending emotion was swamping her. He must have been convinced because he began crooning her name, his hand fumbling with the buttons of her shirt, spreading it open.

He lowered his head and she rolled a little more, her body near rigid with horror and loathing. Her fingers continued the search. She felt no inclination to cry. She felt an overpowering urge to immobilise him.

A stone large enough for her purpose miraculously found its way into her hand when she was certain it was a way off.

How had they ever thought this unstable man was *normal?*
Because he had acted normal, that's why.

His primal jealousy of Ross was the catalyst to set him off.

Somewhere a bird shrieked as though there was need for loud protest.

God forgive me! Samantha thought as she struck out.

Out of the corner of a delirious eye Matt Howarth saw her hand rise. He saw the rock in it. Pain burned through him. She had been pretending after all. His heart broke as she struck him midway between his ear and his temple.

He swayed a little, crumpled on top of her, then as Samantha pushed him off violently, he toppled to the sand.

At first she couldn't stand. She was in shock. She tried again. Fell to her knees. Stood up again. Her face was smarting where he had struck her. The corner of her eye was sore.

Get up, Sam.

A voice inside her head gave the order. Strangely it sounded like her beloved Grandad, long dead. Grandad had been a hero who had gone into a neighbour's burning house to save their small child. As a child, herself, he had been wonderful to her.

Get up, Sam. Run. I'll be with you.

I haven't killed him? Please tell me I haven't killed him.

He's not dead.

Matt was breathing. She brushed her long mane from her hot swollen face. "I'm too weak to stand. Too sick."

Who was she talking to?

No you're not! You'll be fine. Go to the boat.

CHAPTER NINE

THEY came upon a nest down stream in the primal fastness of dense green scrub. It was a good distance from where king tides could sweep the structure away. David set to quickly, photographing the rotting pile of dead leaves, grasses, reeds and other dank vegetation. The mound, some three feet high in the middle was shaped like a pyramid, the circumference of the nest a good thirty feet.

As soon as David was ready Joe parted the pungent rotting vegetation that was generating a considerable amount of heat. He dug down carefully, while Ross kept a watchful eye in case the female crocodile decided to make an early return to the nest. Normally there was a certain excitement in these expeditions but today there was a feeling of restlessness, call it anxiety, about everyone and everything. He for one couldn't wait to get back to the camp. Though he seemed harmless enough Ross didn't have a good opinion of Matt Howarth.

The leathery looking eggs, some fifty or more, about three times the size of a large hen's egg, lay in a rough circle. A good many it might seem, but fewer than 1 per cent of eggs laid resulted in mature crocodiles. Muttering in his own language, very slowly and very carefully Joe prised open a shell already cracked and immediately a tiny little monster, exhibiting all the fierce characteristics of the adult began viciously snapping at his hand.

"Savage little beggar, aren't you!" Joe said fondly, handling the little creature gently. He got his thumb and forefinger behind the neck to hold the belligerent little head still for his photograph. "Stay little fella," he cautioned. "I'll put yah back in the nest soon. Mumma will be back."

David gave a snort of wry laughter and took his shots.

"We should pack it in, David," Ross warned a short time later. "Got all you need?" His waves of anxiety weren't altogether connected with fear of their being overtaken by a man eating croc.

"One more, that's it!" David too had been working under pressure, something gnawing away at him about leaving Sam. Not that there was any real reason for concern. Matt would look after her. He doted on Sam. Nevertheless he, like the others weren't feeling the usual exhilaration. They all wanted to get back to camp.

They broke out of the deep green vine shrouded jungle to an empty clearing where the sun had a pellucid brilliance. Everything glittered in the light. The sandy earth, the rocks, the shining leaves on the banyan trees.

No sign of Samantha or Matt.

Anxiety built up quickly, especially when there was no response to Ross's loud bush call. Only wild duck flew overhead in their curious V shaped formation.

"Where could they be?" Isabelle asked the obvious question, her womanly intuition never to be taken lightly going into overdrive. She knew far too much about needy men. The time bomb ticking on the short fuse. Her heart started to thud against her ribs. "Surely they can't have gone far?"

"Sounds travels. They should have responded to my call. It's rough country out there and its swarming with snakes. I told them to stay put." Ross's light eyes glittered beneath the brim of his akubra.

Joe had walked off studying the flurry of imprints. There was a newly roughed up area, deep depressions in the sandy ground. Within seconds he called to Ross who was already heading towards him. "Two lots, boss," he said quietly.

"Man and a woman moving away," Ross muttered grimly. "They're heading back into the rain forest. *Why?* Surely not to the boat?" His face tightened as his nerves began to jangle. "They would have had the sense to stay put."

"Y'd think so." Joe continued to track ahead, eyes scouting around, even his acute sense of smell coming into play. Towards the line of wild bush the sandy loam hardened, the whole area liberally carpeted with twigs, small and large stones, ankle deep fallen leaves.

"No use wasting time talking." Ross muttered, fighting down an unfamiliar sense of panic. If anything had happened to her! He knew he would barely cope with that.

David and Isabelle joined them, both looking ready for a search. "Looks like they've headed back to the boat," David said, his broad forehead pleated in a frown. "Why the hell would Matt allow it? For that matter Sam has too much common sense. To travel with a guide is one thing but Matt's no bushman. He can't even navigate around Sydney."

"Joe and I will track them down. Don't worry," Ross assured him, feeling a great burden of responsibility.

"Easier said than done, Ross. We'll come too," David was caught up in the general feeling of urgency though Samantha and Matt could wander back at any moment.

To a hot reception he thought as relief inevitably turned to anger. "I've found my way through the jungles of Indonesia," he said, looking grim.

"We can't just stand here," Isabelle said briskly, ranging herself alongside David. "You and Joe take one route, Ross. David and I will take another."

"Co-ee if you find them," Ross instructed her, knowing she would do it anyway. "I can't believe Howarth would be fool enough to go back. And why? They were told to stay put. Anyway let's get cracking. We have to find them while there's sufficient light."

Twenty minutes later he and Joe following signs they were trained to see caught up with Matt Howarth. He was staggering around in a circle, within a bamboo enclosure, obviously disoriented and weary to the bone. It wasn't until they were almost on him that they saw the bloodied caked mess on the side of his head.

"For God's sake, Matt, what happened?" Puzzled, Ross moved swiftly, grasping him by the shoulder with fingers like steel. He wanted to yell what the hell did Howarth think he was doing, but with difficulty he restrained himself. Instead he studied the man's injury. It probably looked worse than it was but for some reason Howarth appeared barely recognisable as though his usual persona had vanished. "Where's Samantha? Where is she?" he asked urgently. "Speak up, man. We're worried sick."

"Stupid bitch!" Matt startled them by saying. He was shivering like he had a fever, cursing incoherently to himself.

Ross couldn't help himself. He rammed the other man against a tree, pinning him to it. "Did you have an argument? Is that it?" he asked fiercely. "Did she go back to the boat?"

Matt braced himself as though expecting to be punched to a pulp. Sweat slicked his entire body. "Little fool hit me." He put a hand to his bulging temple, his hazel eyes dull as stones. "Struck me with a bloody rock."

In the one hundred degree heat Ross's blood turned cold. He made a deep growling sound in his throat, battling a powerful rage. Samantha wouldn't have done such a thing unless Howarth had frightened her. *Threatened* her. His free hand clenched into a fist. The other continued to hold Howarth captive.

Joe jumped a large fallen branch to get to his boss. "Steady, Ross, steady." He put a restraining hand on Ross's shoulder feeling the powerful waves of emotion that were running through his body. "Leave the bugger. Push him out of your mind. We're wasting time. We know Miss Samantha passed through here up to this point."

Suddenly the wild bush looked forbidding and inaccessible. A barred prison to a young woman gently reared in the city. Ross stood rigid beneath the old aboriginal's calming hand. Slowly he pulled himself together. The red tide of rage receded. Every second counted.

"Stay where you are," he snarled at the shaking Howarth in a voice that had to be obeyed without argument or question. "We've marked this spot. Don't move if you value your life."

Matt broke into a spasm of wild laughter, sinking to the vine covered forest floor that was actually alive with insects.

"We're going after Samantha," Ross spoke so harshly Matt's laughter ceased abruptly. "You'd better pray she's okay. If she *isn't,* I just could shoot you, you weak, snivelling coward."

Matt lifted his head, his eyes strangely tragic. "Shoot me. You might as well."

"You're not worth wasting a bullet on." Ross spat out.

They all converged on the river bank within minutes of each other, their journey swift and hard in the oppressive heat.

"No sign of anyone," David yelled. "No Sam. No Matt." He thought they must have missed them completely. God knows any set of tracks would be as good as indistinguishable with so much debris on the forest floor and the undergrowth beneath the forest canopy so thickly screened.

"She's been through here," Joe muttered, knowing exactly how and where to look. "She's no fool. I reckon we'll find her on the boat."

Ross let out a harsh pent up groan, dreading that she might have come to some harm. "Oh God, I hope so, Joe." He felt another terrifying spasm of rage. "If she *is,* she's going to get a good talking to. What the hell went on back there?" His blood burned and he turned away from his old friend abruptly.

"We will see. We will see," Joe soothed him, knowing the terrible upset behind the words of anger. Ross Sunderland had finally found *his* woman.

They all moved towards the jetty, silently praying Samantha would appear on the deck of the boat.

"I think I'll kill Howarth if anything has happened to her." Ross shook his head with a feeling of impotence. "We found Howarth," he called across as the others drew near. "Jabbering to himself in the jungle. Almost incoherent."

"What on earth happened?" David's tongue was like lead in his mouth.

"Samantha must have run away from him." Ross turned, his light eyes blazing. "He pursued her. He's got an almighty lump on his head for his trouble. Apparently she hit him."

David let out a great oath while Isabelle suddenly bent over as though in the sudden grip of severe pain.

Already perturbed, David got an arm around her, supporting her slight weight. "Isabelle!" His voice was a dead giveaway, betraying the depth of his feeling for her. "We travelled too quickly," he groaned. "Isabelle!"

She managed to straighten just as Goldy appeared on deck.

"She's here, she's here!" Goldy yelled, realising how distressed they all were. He waved his arms, beckoning them in. "Where's that bastard, Howarth?" he called. "That's what *I* want to know." Disgustedly Goldy spat on the deck.

"If he's hurt her I'll feed him to the crocodiles," David promised.

Hearing their voices Samantha struggled up from the bunk. She had to think. What could she say? Matt tried to rape her? Something less violent, knowing how they would react to that. Matt had tried to make love to her? Things were getting out of control so she hit him on the head? They wouldn't believe her. Why should they? She had seen the sick passion in Matt's eyes, his mad yearning for her that was almost a blood lust.

He had been determined to have her no matter the consequences.

Her hair was streaming all around her, little bits of twig and dried leaves were still caught in its web it was so thick. She had a red graze on her cheek, numerous little bleeding cuts on her arms from her flight through the forest, the beginnings of what would be a colourful black eye from when Matt had struck her.

You've got to face them, Sammy. You are no way to blame.

Grandad again. He'd always called her *Sammy*. Hadn't he shown her which way to run?

When she made it on deck they all stared at her as though rooted to the spot.

"My God!" Ross paled beneath his tan, a hard glitter in his eyes, his face a graven mask.

"Oh, Sam," Isabelle who had been expecting something bad, nevertheless burst into heart broken tears, realising as only an abused woman could what Samantha had endured.

"Samantha, sweetheart!" For a big man David closed the distance between them as nimbly as a cat. He drew his sister into his arms, hugging her thankfully to him. "You're okay? Tell me," he whispered, shutting his mind against the worst.

"Yes, yes," she reassured him quickly. "A bit knocked about."

"He's going to pay for this," he gritted. "How could I have taken such a viper into our midst?"

Ross did his best to comfort his distraught sister. Belle had been so stoical right through her own tragedy, yet the sight of a battered Samantha had unleashed an uncontrollable tide of grief. A delayed reaction? Fellow feeling?

Hearing Isabelle's pitifully sobbing, Samantha entirely forgot her own woes. Gently she broke away from David's embrace moving across the deck to her friend's side. "Belle, dear, I'm okay. Really I am." After one brief searing glance, Samantha averting her eyes from Ross standing on the other side of Isabelle, so tall and dauntingly remote. "I'm so sorry I gave you all such a fright." She put her arm comfortingly around Isabelle's narrow waist, herself upset by the misery that contorted Isabelle's beautiful features. "Come with me, Belle. We both need rest."

Isabelle, still sobbing, went willingly.

The men watched in silence for a while. "Well she's safe," Ross muttered finally.

"Howarth still has to be dealt with," David said. His strongly hewn face took on a disquieting cast.

"I'll go back for him," Ross said.

"Risky the way you feel." David gave a grim smile.

"I'll go with you, Boss," Joe, on the point of exhaustion, volunteered.

"I'd rather you stay here, Joe," Ross said, gripping his old friend's arm. "I think you've done enough for one day."

"No matter." Joe shook his snow white head.

"If you're worried I might harm him in some way, I give you my word I won't. Or not much."

"I'll come with you," David said decisively. "We can keep a brake on one another. Besides, you'll need another pair of strong hands, Ross. Sam's okay. I can tell. She always was a feisty little thing. It's Isabelle who appears to be in the greater pain."

"I'll watch over them Boss," Joe promised. "I'll see they're both all right. You watch over yourselves, okay?"

"S'truth! I need a drink," Goldy said hoarsely. "I hadn't counted on this. A beer for you, Joe?"

Joe nodded. "I reckon."

Ross and David swiftly exited the boat, pounding down the jetty. What it was to be young and strong as a bull buffalo, Joe thought. He'd been like that in the old days. He watched as they disappeared into the olive green line of wild scrub. Whether Howarth was going to cop a few punches or not Joe knew he wouldn't want to be in the sick bugger's shoes.

* * *

Nothing was the same any more. That one ugly incident changed everything. They all returned to Darwin. Ross and David took charge of the disgraced but queerly unrepentant Matt Howarth, dropping him off at the hospital where he was subjected to a thorough physical and mental evaluation. On no account had Samantha wanted to press charges. Not for Matt's sake—he deserved no consideration—but for her brother's and her own. The story would inevitably make the newspapers. She couldn't have that. She wanted to blot the whole thing out. Matt would never come near her again. She prayed he would never harass another young woman but his fixation appeared to have been solely with her.

As it turned out Matt had a medical record going way back. He had been diagnosed bipolar in his late teens, a diagnosis re-affirmed after he'd had his nervous breakdown. According to his own account he had been on and off his medication ever since, citing negative side effects he couldn't tolerate. The only problem was he had difficulty controlling his behaviour when off it. How he had sustained his injury—which Samantha was grateful had proved not all that serious—was skirted over. He had become disoriented in the bush, remembered falling over, crashing into something hard. Maybe a rock. In the absence of a conflicting account, his was accepted.

David despite his intense anger and feelings of self blame waited around Darwin just long enough to see his flawed protégé out of hospital, complete with medication and into a motel where he was left to get on with his own life.

"So you never want to see me again. Is that it?" Matt, incredibly, appeared to think of *himself* as the victim.

"Much better that way, Matt," David told him, keeping his face expressionless when so much anger, disappointment and disgust, was upon him. "You abused Samantha's trust. My trust. It could all have ended very badly only my gutsy sister was able to limit the damage. I wouldn't show my face around the Territory again. Get your things together and clear out. Take good advice. Stay on your medication. This is Sunderland's part of the world. No way has he forgiven you. In fact we've decided it's safer if he doesn't come near you. Come anywhere near Samantha again and you'll answer to us both."

It was Joe who drove Isabelle and Samantha back to North Star while Ross and David turned the film already shot in for scanning and tied up a number of loose ends. No way could anyone pretend they had the same enthusiasm for the project. Matt's brutish behaviour had shocked them all. They needed to mark time for a while. Perhaps when David came back from Indonesia where he had a long-time commitment.

A big perhaps!

Samantha had the dismal feeling Ross would never consent to her joining another expedition. In fact it seemed like it was all over for them so withdrawn had he been in the wake of Matt's attack. No words of comfort for her. He *couldn't* be blaming her for what had happened.

Isabelle had tried to console her. "How could you think such a thing, Samantha? I think it struck my brother hard, if anything had happened to you…!" She left the rest unsaid as though Samantha only had to open her eyes wide enough to see the reasons for Ross's seemingly perverse reactions.

After almost a week the men returned home while Isabelle and Samantha, closer than sisters, ran together to greet them. Samantha went to her brother first who slipped an arm around her waist and hugged her. They had spoken daily, sometimes twice daily on the phone so she was up to date on everything that was happening.

"Ross?" Finally she turned to him, her eyes searching his darkly handsome face.

"Hi." He acknowledged her. No smile, but a piercing, comprehensive gaze, noting no doubt how quickly she had healed. "How are you?"

"Fine."

He nodded approval. They went forward to the front steps of the homestead.

Behind them David reached out a long arm for Isabelle who seemed to float into what could only be interpreted as an embrace. He couldn't prevent himself. He kissed her cheek, inhaling the lovely natural fragrance of her skin and immediately drew back. This woman affected him like great music affected him. She touched his heart and his mind and his soul. "I didn't like to be away from you both," he told her quietly. "You were so terribly upset before we left. How are you now?"

"Much better." She smiled up at him, recognising and accepting she loved this man. Whatever the outcome. It wasn't something she had asked for, or something she felt she deserved. It was Fate. Just having him beside her was enough. He was so powerful yet so gentle. She revelled in his bearing, so close to *regal* it didn't matter but absolutely natural. If only such a man had entered her life before Blair! *If only...if only.* The journey through life was paved with *if onlys.* But what an enormous difference that would have made. She would have been spared so many ugly experiences. She would have been able to act more openly. Often over the last few days she had come to the brink of telling Samantha of the brutality of her short marriage but at the last moment drawn back. Why heap all that on Samantha's graceful shoulders? Samantha was carrying her own burden and carrying it well.

Without thinking Isabelle caught David's large handsome hand linking her fingers through his. He looked down at the beautiful face at his shoulder, drawing in a sharp breath. This one small gesture he found terribly important like a long awaited message. On a wave of elation he bent his tawny head over hers saying in a low, telling voice: "God, I've missed you."

"I've missed *you.*" She let out a long fragmented sigh, the faintest flicker of *fear* could it possibly be? in her luminous upward glance. He couldn't understand it, but whatever it was it was unbearably moving.

He lifted her slender fingers and kissed them gently. If there was a direct way to this woman's heart he was going to find it.

They ate dinner in the breakfast room, carrying their steaming fragrant coffee out onto the rear terrace where the great copper moon of the tropics lit up the garden and illuminated the seating area with its attractive rattan furniture. David and Isabelle kept the conversation going. Ross from time to time joined in.

The great talk of the Outback at that time was not just the death of a legendary Territory figure and cattle baron, Rigby Kingston, but the shock distribution of his will. All the Territory knew there were skeletons in the Kingston closet; Kingston's elder son and heir had been killed a decade or so before in a light aircraft crash which for a time had caused murmurs and it now came as a shock that Kingston's granddaughter Alexandra had been nominated chief beneficiary. Overnight she had become an heiress and a prime candidate for one of the most eligible young women in the country. Still it was impossible for most people to imagine a slip of a girl would be able to take over the running of a vast station like Moondai, much less want to if she was anything like her social butterfly of a mother.

"Daniel's not going away in a hurry," Ross said briskly, referring to Moondai's highly rated overseer, Daniel Carson, Kingston's former right hand man and not yet thirty. "He'll hold the fort until a good professional manager can be found. That's if Daniel doesn't want to stay on."

Isabelle nodded agreement. "I remember Alexandra as a little girl," she said with warmth. "She was a great little rider, won quite a few prizes, something of a tomboy, her father adored her."

The subject of the Kingstons was gradually dropped; another picked up. Ross launched into a story about the "man with the Midas touch," another rich Territory tycoon called Moreland. Samantha was reminded how the Outback seemed to breed men that were larger than life. Small wonder she thought. Such men were the descendants of the early pioneers and settlers; men who had overcome every obstacle the vast, dangerous, inspiring and heartbreaking Territory, the last frontier, could throw at them. Against all the odds they had not only survived but gone on to found dynasties.

She rested her head back, conscious nostalgia mixed with a strange exhaustion was working its way through her veins like a drug. She knew Ross was deliberately maintaining a front, but that wondrous tangible connection that had been between them appeared to have been broken. David and Isabelle on the other hand radiated a *togetherness* that was quite striking. They didn't have to tell her they were in love. That was as plain to see as the moon that sailed above them. She couldn't really see how Isabelle had fallen deeply in love so soon after the death of her husband. Obviously it wasn't something Isabelle had *wanted*. As had happened in her own case both of them appeared to have surrendered to a kind of biological demand. Nevertheless she was very happy for Isabelle and her much loved brother. They seemed to have been made for each other. As for her and Ross? She had chosen a far stormier path.

David's voice drew her out of her reverie.

"…well we can pursue the possibilities," she heard him say. "What do you think, Sam?"

"I'm sorry." She had to clear her throat. "I must have drifted off. What was it you were saying?"

"It doesn't matter, pet," David said kindly.

She touched her hand to her temple. "I have a slight headache. It's the heat."

"We're due for a storm," Isabelle predicted. Certainly it was on the air. Already clouds were ringing the moon.

"If it's okay with you all, I think I'll have an early night." She was apologetic.

Ross glanced over at her. "Why don't we go for a walk?" he suggested. "The night air might shift it. It's much too early to turn in." His glance cut sideways to David, certain David wanted desperately to be alone with Isabelle.

"Okay," she answered gracefully, determined not to run away from him.

Ross put out his hand. She let him take it. No way was she going to allow him to upset her. She had to speak to him. Draw him out into the open. Only then would she know what she had to do.

No sooner were they on the path than he let go of her hand.

"What's wrong between us, Ross?" She plunged right in. "Clearly something is."

"Well if that doesn't take the prize," he groaned, his vibrant voice was strained. "Howarth bloody near raped you and I'm supposed not only to let him get away with it but forget about it?" Couldn't she understand how a man felt when his woman was attacked? It had torn the heart out of him and caused such a harsh reaction. But that was him. His love for her had drawn him in too deep.

"*I* have to," Samantha protested. "So how is it *my* fault?"

"I never said it was your fault," he answered curtly, his nostrils flaring. Inside he was lit up with an enormous rage, powerless and frustrated that he wasn't able to make Howarth pay for attempting a crime he could have got away with. He was angry with Samantha too for giving him the greatest fright of his life. She had only stayed with Howarth to pique him never dreaming Howarth would try to hurt her. He had to shut out that dreadful scene as he had imagined it, before it drove him mad.

"Well you've retreated from me, haven't you?" Samantha was saying. "You've gone away. Do you do this often? Get a woman to fall headlong in love with you. Fall in love yourself but can't sustain it."

"Stop talking nonsense," he said bluntly, feeling absolutely hellish.

"I'm talking commitments, Ross," she retorted, flaring up. Both of them were incredibly on edge. "That's not nonsense. I thought what we had was *real*. Very serious."

He stopped in the middle of the path, his lean muscular body in silhouette against the moonlight. "When the woman you love is attacked by another man it cuts into the deepest most primitive part of you. Surely you can understand that?"

She stared up at him, aware of his tormented expression. "I do. I *do*, Ross. It was terrible what happened but it could have been so much worse."

"Isn't that what I'm saying," he retorted bleakly and continued walking. "You never have said just how far he got?"

What had been hazy was now clear. "Ah, Ross, are you doubting my word?"

He was wracked with powerful emotions. "I just don't think I could live with it."

Hot tears sprang into her eyes. "Would I have lost my value?" Her tone spoke volumes. "I'm sullied. I'm spoiled? Is that it?"

"You don't know what you're saying, or I'm not communicating what I feel," he gritted, feeling like he was shut in a cage and couldn't get out. "I can't come to terms with Howarth getting away with it. The punishment should match the crime. Or the attempted crime. He was on the brink of it when presumably you hit him?"

"I had no option, Ross," she said. "You got a few punches in, I believe." David had told her.

"So I did. Do you blame me? The sick bastard had absolutely no remorse. It was as though he had a *right* to do what he did. I know a guy who suffers from bipolar disorder. A nice guy. A hard worker. No way would he act like that. Howarth is plain crazy."

"So what did you want to do, *kill* him?" she asked raggedly, her emotions getting the better of her.

His face hardened. He turned away from her. "Very much so, except I'd have to come down to the level of the beast. Sometimes it's hard fitting into the dictates of civilised society, Samantha."

Her heart ached so much she felt like weeping. They were drifting so far apart. "I'm so sorry, Ross."

He let out a frustrated breath. "Your being sorry makes no sense. You were the *victim*."

A breeze loaded with ozone floated around their heated bodies, but it didn't damp down the fierce emotions. "He got no further than some awful slobbering kisses and he touched my breasts," she confessed, painfully, aware he was desperate to *know* the extent of the attack. "I *had* to act passive. I *had* to let him until I found some kind of weapon. Even though he was trying to do the unthinkable I didn't want to kill him. I wanted to disable him so I could get away."

"You were very brave." She had earned his respect. But he was still angry with her as though she had failed some test. What was the matter with him, for Chrissake! She was the innocent victim. There were always men like Howarth. He was sickened and horrified even when he wanted to treat her so tenderly. He could see the glint of her tears.

Love was terrible.

He couldn't think of a life without her. Yet his anger was driving her away when he should have been embracing her. He had to be insane.

"I wasn't brave." Samantha shook her head in denial. "I was charged with adrenaline. I don't like being the powerless female."

"I think we can now all safely say you're not." He sighed deeply in the darkness. "You're telling me the truth about this? All of it?"

She waited a moment to compose herself, a dismal melancholy well and truly descended upon her. "I'd be a truly remarkable woman had I been damaged further and was still able to function the way I have since. My whole heart goes out to rape victims. It's an unspeakable ordeal. The fallout goes way beyond a violated body right to a woman's soul."

He groaned in empathy. "Which was *precisely* why I felt like killing Howarth. His lack of remorse was the most unforgivable part. I can't help wondering if you should have pressed charges?"

Warily she looked at him. "Would you have wanted that?"

"I would have stood by your decision," he said firmly. "It's like I've said. These sort of crimes—intended crimes in his case—shouldn't go unpunished."

"Ross, I had to make the decision I thought in the best interests of us all. I wanted to avoid the notoriety." Her voice cracked. "Besides, the deciding factor was, I got away."

He laughed angrily, frustration a knife in his guts. He knew it had been a bad, *bad* idea to leave her. "What a miracle that was. Not only did you get away from Howarth who in his manic state was hard enough for David and me to control. You found your way through the jungle. I mean you know *nothing* about the bush. Inexperienced stock men sometimes get lost."

"My Grandad showed me the way," she said, praying he wouldn't reject such a notion scornfully. "Grandad was always there for me when my dad wasn't. Grandad was talking to me the whole time."

"Samantha!"

The sudden solicitude in his voice brought the tears to her eyes. He wasn't openly sceptical. He merely sounded…indulgent. "He really did," she said. "Grandad reaffirmed what I believe. Death isn't the end for us. We move on to a different dimension. I wasn't hysterical. I realise you might think that. I was sick and shaken but I had my goal firmly in mind. I did what Grandad told me. I made it back to the boat."

He let out a long suffering sigh. He had relived her flight through the jungle many times. Marvelled she had found her way out. It looked as though she had had help. "Well incredible as it may seem we have your Grandad to thank for that."

"You don't believe it?"

He gave the ghost of a smile. "Maybe. What's important is *you* do." He put out his hand in reconciliation but for some reason she couldn't begin to explain to herself Samantha went into retreat. She jerked back, too close to disintegrating. "The old servants' entrance is over there, Ross," she said, turning her head. "I really do have a headache. I'm going to bed."

David and Isabelle lingered on the terrace, in their armchairs, each basking in the glow of happiness the other gave them. Isabelle for her part felt like she was emerging like a butterfly all velvety and new from her spent cocoon.

"Ross is pretty upset," David remarked eventually. "The whole incident with Howarth shocked him to the core. Not that anyone could blame him. A man would do *anything* to protect and defend the women he loves."

She fixed her eyes on the arching sprays of some flowering orchids. How beautiful they were. How serene. "Not all men are like that," she said. *Don't panic. There's absolutely nothing to panic about. This is David.*

He wouldn't be judgmental.

Her tone was so serious he seized on it. "You've known someone like that?" He turned his chair slightly, so he could face her directly.

She was done with pretence. This was the man she loved. She had to be entirely honest with him. "I was married to one," she told him as quietly as if she were talking to herself.

"Isabelle!" He reached out and took her hands. "What are you saying?"

She gave a sad smile, staring down at their locked hands. "Nothing thousands, maybe millions of women couldn't say. I was in an abusive marriage, David. That's why I went to pieces when I saw what Howarth had done to Sam."

"My God!" His expression turned stony. No wonder Ross had been boiling with rage. All set to pummel Howarth into the ground when he had urged some restraint. "Do you want to tell me about it?"

"I have to."

"Come here to me." He saw the stricken look on her face. He stood; gathered her up like a defenceless small girl and carried her back to the huge bucket chair where he could cradle her.

She placed her head in the hollow of his chest, drawing heavily on the comfort he gave her. "I've never been able to tell anyone else—not my dear father nor my brother. I was too ashamed. Too worried what they might do. You see how Ross has reacted to Samantha's trauma. He's traumatised himself. I trust you, David."

"You're *right* to," he said, kissing her hair. He was enormously grateful she had decided to liberate herself from her dark secret. And with *him*.

"In a way you've healed me." She curled into him like a long lost rescued child. "I know I don't look like a woman who would tolerate physical and mental abuse but I'm ashamed to say I was. At least for some time. It didn't start until six or seven months into our marriage then everything started to go wrong. No one could have been more jealous or possessive than Blair. We were out practically every night of the week. He acted like he adored me, but I couldn't do a thing right. The abuse started the moment we set foot inside our door. The first time he hit me I was shocked out of my mind. I couldn't believe it. I was married to a batterer. Who could believe it? He'd been so charming, so loving and considerate throughout our courtship. He didn't *look* like a man who could abuse his wife. Most people thought I was extremely lucky to have married him."

"My God!" David had heard all those stories. Had even given them credence.

"Afterwards—after these episodes—he appeared to be genuinely sick with shame. He showered me with presents. Promised he'd never do it again. Of course he did. Gradually I began to hit back. It was all so degrading."

"My poor Isabelle!" he groaned, feeling shame for his own sex. Men *were* the aggressors. It was a miracle she hadn't wound up dead. And to think Hartmann had fooled everyone with the Mr. Nice Guy persona. There was a parallel with Matt. Some men really did lead double lives.

Isabelle lay against David's powerful muscular chest, hearing the rhythmic thud of his heart. "He told me if I tried to leave him he would kill me."

"What miserable cowards these men are!" He released a long breath. "Isabelle, you really should have told someone. Your father or after he was gone, Ross."

"I'm *never* going to tell Ross," she shuddered. "He wouldn't believe I couldn't turn to him for help. Think how upset he is about Sam. I was too proud, David. Too unwilling to admit I'd made a terrible mistake. Another thing, I'm not going to burden Ross with what happened to me. I love him too much. But I can't pretend with *you*." Her voice trembled with emotion.

"Because I'm going to be your lover, your husband?" he said with a sense of the inevitability of it all. This woman was infinitely precious.

"Do you want to be?" She couldn't look at him. She had to *feel* his response.

"Want to be?" he echoed, the longing he felt for her welling up. "I've waited this long. Not a second more. Kiss me, Isabelle," he said, masterfully. He lowered his head, his blood *glittering* there was so much passion, unerringly finding her lovely upturned mouth.

Desire took his breath away. Desire mixed with a kind of agony. How much horror had she endured, this exquisite creature? The reason why she had dissolved into heart breaking sobs on the boat was fully explained.

Nothing remotely like this had ever happened to Isabelle before. The boldness, the sweetness, the flavour of real passion. She had grown used to Blair calling her frigid. Kissing had never been like this with Blair, even at the best of times before they were married. Even the early on sex didn't come near it. This was sensual bliss, for the moment all-consuming.

They held each other as if drowning in a sea of rapture, each unable to get enough of the other. Kisses without pause. Sublime kisses when two lovers passed into a brand new world of their own.

"Will you?" David's strong hand trembled over the curve of her breast. "Will you marry me? I know it's not long since...since." He found himself unable to speak Hartmann's name he felt such repugnance. "You deserve happiness, Isabelle. No waiting. No fake mourning period. You *escaped*. You deserve the right man to love you. I swear I'll spend my whole life making it up to you. I love you, Isabelle. Something momentous happened to me the moment I laid eyes on you."

"And me." She placed her hand along his cheek, close to weeping with joy.

"You'll come to Indonesia with me?" he urged, looking into her beautiful eyes.

"I'll come to the ends of the world with you," she said simply.

"My *love*," he answered, profoundly moved.

"Stay with me tonight," she begged, taking a few shallow breaths just to calm herself.

"Is it what you truly want? You're not saying it to please me?"

"To please *me*." She gave a broken laugh and spread her fingers lovingly along his strong jawline. Her David. Her lion. "I love you, David," she said, speaking with her whole heart.

"What have I done to deserve you?" he swiftly countered. "What was it you told that cowardly cur you married that sent him storming out of the party?"

She drew a jagged breath. "I was cruel."

"Don't!" He rejected that entirely. "You couldn't be."

She shuddered. "I told him that I was leaving him that very night. I wasn't coming home. I'd made arrangements I would never come back to him and if he threatened me I'd go to the police, his boss, his mother, his family, everyone he knew and tell them what sort of man he really was. Something about me must have convinced him I really meant it. Had I told him when we were alone in our home I'd have risked my life."

His heart contracted at a possible truth. "Instead you started to get your life on track."

"With Blair out of the way, yes. I'm as sure as I can be, he didn't intend suicide," she said. "I've thought and thought about it. He *had* to live to fight another day. Such was his tormented nature he wasn't going to give me up. We were both destined to live in a dark, dangerous secret world. His death was an accident."

"And you're asking me to keep what sort of man he was a secret?" He tilted her chin, made her raise her eyes to his. "I don't know if I can do that, Isabelle. My role is to protect and defend you."

"But Ross would know," she said sounding distressed about it.

"Ross will internalise it and understand," he said firmly. "You had found the courage to leave Hartmann. Personally I'd like to shut a few people up. For a start that appalling woman Evelyn Hartmann. No one is going to spread false rumours about my wife. You have to leave it to me now, Isabelle. Will you?"

In the half light his eyes glowed golden. "Yes, David," she said.

CHAPTER TEN

THE storm broke with tremendous power some time after midnight. Such was its savagery Samantha felt a shuddering wave of panic. Storms could be extremely destructive leaving people to not only mop up their homes but their lives. She rose from her bed where she'd been tossing and turning fretfully, to go to the high arched doors that led onto the verandah. She literally jumped as thunder rolled across the heavens then broke asunder with a tremendous cracking noise like forest giants being felled. The tall pier mirror behind her turned a blazing silver, reflecting the electrical power of the lightning bolt that drove through the highly charged atmosphere to plant its spearhead in the shuddering earth.

She padded out onto the verandah in her bare feet, drawing back almost instantly as the rain came down, suddenly chilling and remorseless. Its deep throated roar seemed to her excited imagination like an army on the march. The wind *shrieked* above it. The force of it almost took her breath away. She couldn't imagine what it would be like in a cyclone. Terrifying! She dared not go near the balustrade. Rain enveloped the immediate world. Driving walls of water that almost immediately began to challenge the guttering of the huge roof. It didn't seem possible the guttering could handle such a massive volume of water. She had a nightmare moment when she thought the roof could collapse.

The hem of her nightgown, lifted, fluttered, whipped around her body, already soaked. Not that she cared. The power of the storm was so mesmerising even as she trembled before nature at its most frightening and majestic she continued to stare out in thrall, her vision periodically seared by the great jagged flashes of lightning. This side of the homestead had to be exposed to the worst of the lashing. Sheets of water drove across the verandah intimidating her to the point where she fell back against the shutters. She didn't want to close them against the spectacular theatre of the storm, but she would have to before the rain entered the bedroom. It was utterly black out there. Black and silver. To be out in the storm's fury!

"Samantha?"

Even through the cacophony she heard his voice. She wasn't dreaming. She turned her head in its direction, her heart heaving a great surge of elation at the sight of his tall hard muscled figure striding along the verandah towards her. All she had wanted was for him to come to her.

Yet his manner was far from loverlike. "What the hell are you doing?" he demanded, gathering her up and drawing her back forcibly into the shelter of the bedroom. "Don't you know when a storm is in full swing you can be struck by lightning?"

"What?" she asked dazedly. "It comes in under the roof?"

"You bet your life it does. Lightning can reach you if you're standing in front of a window *inside* a house. I just knew you'd be out here lapping up the pyrotechnics."

"Well, they're pretty impressive aren't they?" Her nerves were screaming like the wind. Excitement whipped up in her at a tremendous rate, fraught with sexuality. She had him all to herself, quite alone in her lovely bedroom. She had to make the most of it. She had to get through to this complex man that she *loved* him. That no secrets were hidden from him. They could make a good life together.

"You're wet." He ran his hands in a near frenzy down her

slick arms, his proximity to her rendering him as weak as Samson shorn of his mane.

"So are you," she stood on tiptoe to whisper into his face. "Who cares?"

"I have to close the shutters," he said tersely, turning his dark head, a man drunk on beauty. Dazzled by it. "At least for a while. We'll have to make do with the ceiling fan."

"You're going to *stay* with me? I thought you'd decided it was time for me to get out of your life?"

"Don't start," he gritted, already on razor edge. She shouldn't tease him when he felt this way, strung out with yearning, his blood roaring in his veins.

"Don't close them yet," she begged. "Let's watch."

"Then I'll hold you." His hand closed tightly over her shoulders as a fierce white light lit up the world. Rain streamed across the broad verandah. "A minute more." He couldn't help but understand her excitement. Her excitement was his. And much more. It was a provocation, almost a directive to action he couldn't ignore.

"Just the two of us together." She smiled back up at him, a smile that drew him like the moon draws the tides.

"Didn't you call me?" he challenged tautly, doing as desire commanded. He turned her fully into his arms, pressing her wet body against his, consumed up by his own arousal.

The stimulation was *violent*. His blood heated to sizzling point. There she stood within his embrace, near naked except for a froth of silk. Wet silk he could so easily rip from her. The passion for her he had been holding under such tight rein broke loose like a wild stallion that would not be controlled.

The rain was heavier now. Deafening. He groaned softly, feeling the answering tension in her body, painful, *sublime*, tension as great as his own. She seemed to have lost weight since her ordeal. He could feel her nipples flooded with blood hard as berries against the palms of his hands. Her breasts were smaller he thought taking their delicate weight. The

heat in his body rose to a fever. He could feel her ribs through
her satin skin. He let his hands slide down to her narrow
waist, over the curve of her hips and thighs unable to stop
himself from directing his caresses to the heart shaped apex
of her body.

"Do you want me?" she whispered, drawing a shuddering
breath.

"I want to keep you forever," he muttered almost fiercely into
her neck. "I'll *show* you!"

Energy seethed and snapped around him like blue burning
electricity. The storm was forgotten. He was bewitched. With
one movement he pushed the wet nightgown down from her
shoulders, letting it pool at their feet.

An elemental flash of lightning picked her out like a spot-
light. She looked *exquisite*. Lovely luminous face. Beautiful
small breasts, rosebud nipples, tapering waist, delicate hips, sex
hidden by wisps of gold, slender sculpted legs, high arched feet.

"Samantha," he breathed, lowering his mouth to hers while
she swayed into him, twining her arms around his waist.

Passion poured into her so she felt her legs would give way.
She clung to him as though he was all there was in a rocket-
ing world.

"My most beautiful Samantha."

Her breath caught. How the passion and the tenderness in
his voice worked on her! The bloodrush to her extremities!

His tongue was filling and exploring her mouth. She opened
it wider to receive such ecstasy.

"You want to torture me, do you?" he muttered strangely.

"Never! I want to love you." She felt weaker and weaker,
sinking deeper into his embrace. The fierce tug of contractions
began deep in her womb. The pain and the pleasure. His mouth
was taking her very soul.

Roughly, his movements spurred by his desperate passion
and all the little exciting sounds that issued from her throat he
lifted her effortlessly and walked back to the bed and deep

shadows. In sheer abandon he threw her onto the tumbled bed watching her roll away from him across the coverlet.

That would never do. He wanted the two of them together. Fused. As one. He wanted her to open her heart and her mind and her body to him.

Another clap of thunder bombarded the house. They heard it but it didn't distract them.

"Why have I got my clothes off when you've got yours on?" She lifted herself onto one elbow. "Come close to me, Ross. Please come. I want you so badly. I hate it when you're angry with me."

How shamed he suddenly was. "Not angry with *you*. Angry with myself. I've had demons to fight."

"Then let me help you." She held out her arms.

"You're a sorceress!" Her body was glistening like a pearl.

"*Your* sorceress. No one else's."

"Then you'll have to prove it," he said a little raggedly. He stripped off his shirt and sat on the side of the bed.

She was eager to help rid him of his clothes, coming behind him and laying her heated face against the breadth of his back. Not satisfied she inched closer spreading her slender legs to encircle his hips. "I love you madly." She rained kisses on his velvety skin, loving the very smell of him, the glowing masculinity.

"*Aaah!*" His breath seeped from him in a long voluptuous sigh. He threw back his head back, revelling in her attentions. After a moment she rose up onto her knees, leaning against him. "Do you love me? I know at first you didn't. You didn't even *like* me."

He turned his head so their mouths could meet. "Liking didn't even enter it," he told her moments later when she was lying across his lap. "I wanted you from the moment I laid eyes on you. As well you know."

"Do you remember our first kiss?" She would remember it for centuries.

"I'm still marvelling," he exclaimed as he stood, turning her over onto the bed. He was seized by the desire to be as naked as she was. "You don't think I'm going to let you tease me all night?" he asked, staring down at her.

"I love to tease you." Fever flooded in. Sweet intoxicating fever.

"Well I've *come* for you," he said. Swiftly he stripped off the rest of his clothing and stood before her, a marvellous looking man his erection full and hard.

"Now's *my* time," he murmured in the deepest, most seductive voice. He sank onto the bed, pulling her in his arms, immersing himself in her fragrance. "Oh God, that's *so* good," he groaned. "Just to touch you is to solve all my problems in one swoop. I love you, Samantha," he said with boundless tenderness.

Her heart jumped into her throat. "Repeat that please."

"I love you." His tone was even more darkly erotic.

"And I love *you!*" She hugged him closer, insides melting, her joy was so extreme.

"Go on," he commanded. "Tell me. I'm your perfect mate."

"You *are!*" She let her hands move luxuriously over him in perfect freedom. "No other man in the world will do."

"That's good, because I cannot, *will not,* share. You're mine."

He held her face to him and Samantha's eyelids fluttered then closed.

It seemed to him he was *starving,* ravenous for sex with this *one* woman favoured above all others. All other thoughts, all the impotent rage that had given him hell all week fell away. They were *together.* That was all that mattered. The world was washed clean.

His hungry mouth began a long voluptuous slide down over her body, opalescent in the semi-dark. "Trust me, do you?" Quickly he raised his head.

"With my life." Her fingers sank into his thick curling hair. Emotional tears sprang to her eyes, as all her senses heightened into an exquisite, excruciating awareness.

"That's good, because I want you for life," said he tautly. "I've struck gold, Samantha, with you. I'll never give you up."

"As long as we both shall live?" She put all pretence aside.

He was still for a moment, his face resting against her thigh. "Yes." It was said very quietly but it resonated like a vow.

"Then that's all I could ask."

Outside the tumult of the storm grew less and less. The distant roar of thunder began to fade away. Every tree, every shrub, every flower to the blades of grass glistened and glinted with rain. A crush of scents entered the room. Petals, aromatic herbs, exotic fruits.

Out of love and need, their courtship continued to undeniable delight and it had to be said, growing frustrations. Spread eagled on the bed, Samantha couldn't stifle her tiny, high pitched moans. The teasing was so exquisite it was quite simply an agony. Once she tried to speak but instead exhaled deeply, the hollow of her back arching up from the bed as he tongued her most secret place.

Sensation flared into flames miles high.

"If anything happened to you I don't think life would mean anything to me." He lifted a face taut with passion. "Do you *know* what that's like for a man?"

"But how could I replace you?" Samantha spoke up, though she couldn't seem to get her voice above a whisper. "I've told you what you are. You're *everything* to me."

"Then we ought to get married." He stated what he so fervently wanted.

Samantha's eyes went wide. She lay there, stunned, speechless for the moment beyond her. Then a tremulous query, "Ross?"

"I thought I was making that clear, my dearest heart," he said gently. "I'll make it formal. Will you marry me, Samantha Langdon? Will you become my beloved wife?"

She repeated the wondrous words like they were the lyrics of the most beautiful love song every composed.

"Yes, marry." He laughed at her reaction, rising up so his

powerful torso was suspended above her, supported by his strong arms. "You're not allowed to say no."

"Would I dare?" She gave a little broken laugh, rapture pulsing through her making her entire body glow.

"Not if you're longing for more love making, you won't!"

"Then it's yes!" Everything about her bespoke her delight. "Yes, yes, yes."

"Perfect." He allowed himself to collapse full length beside her, turning again on his side to face her. "Then that's settled."

"Not yet," she whispered. "Continuing to make love to me was part of the bargain."

"Which of course I intend to honour." He wound her long hair around his fist. "So...first your face—" he caressed, stroked, kissed her face all over "—then your neck....no, I'm rushing things...your lovely mouth..." Long moments later... "Your breasts...how the nipples flare to my touch...the curve of your stomach, so smooth..." More kisses that moved downwards. Exquisite. But they soothed her not at all.

"Come to me," she begged, her limbs flailing in mounting ecstasy.

"Don't cry."

"I'm not crying." But she was. "Please..." Her voice trailed off as he took hold of her body and entered her powerfully.

Two bodies. One flesh. A ritual when performed with love that is indeed a consecration.

Outside in the rain washed sky the moon made its reappearance from behind a bank of clouds as if on cue. It shone far into that enchanted night. On Isabelle and David, asleep now after making love with such tenderness and mutual adoration. Isabelle on her side, her dark head pillowed on his shoulder, David on his back with one arm draped protectively around her.

On Samantha and Ross lost in the magic of their passionate coupling.

Fate had brought them all together. Their entwined futures were thus laid out. The moon, a fabulous illumination in the dark wind tossed night, was witness to that.

* * * * *

Look for Alexandra's story.
Coming soon.

If you enjoyed what you just read,
then we've got an offer you can't resist!

Take 2 bestselling love stories FREE!

Plus get a FREE surprise gift!

Clip this page and mail it to Harlequin Reader Service®

IN U.S.A.	IN CANADA
3010 Walden Ave.	P.O. Box 609
P.O. Box 1867	Fort Erie, Ontario
Buffalo, N.Y. 14240-1867	L2A 5X3

YES! Please send me 2 free Harlequin Romance® novels and my free surprise gift. After receiving them, if I don't wish to receive anymore, I can return the shipping statement marked cancel. If I don't cancel, I will receive 6 brand-new novels every month, before they're available in stores! In the U.S.A., bill me at the bargain price of $3.57 plus 25¢ shipping & handling per book and applicable sales tax, if any*. In Canada, bill me at the bargain price of $4.05 plus 25¢ shipping & handling per book and applicable taxes**. That's the complete price and a savings of 10% off the cover prices—what a great deal! I understand that accepting the 2 free books and gift places me under no obligation ever to buy any books. I can always return a shipment and cancel at any time. Even if I never buy another book from Harlequin, the 2 free books and gift are mine to keep forever.

186 HDN DZ72
386 HDN DZ73

Name	(PLEASE PRINT)
Address	Apt.#
City	State/Prov. Zip/Postal Code

Not valid to current Harlequin Romance® subscribers.
Want to try another series? Call 1-800-873-8635
or visit www.morefreebooks.com.

* Terms and prices subject to change without notice. Sales tax applicable in N.Y.
** Canadian residents will be charged applicable provincial taxes and GST.
    All orders subject to approval. Offer limited to one per household.
® are registered trademarks owned and used by the trademark owner or its licensee.

HROM04R   ©2004 Harlequin Enterprises Limited

HARLEQUIN *Presents*

Welcome to a world filled with passion, romance and royals!

Royal Brides

The Scorsolini Princes: Proud rulers and passionate lovers who need convenient wives!

HIS ROYAL LOVE-CHILD

by Lucy Monroe

June 2006

Danette Michaels knew that there would be no marriage or future as Principe Marcello Scorsolini's secret mistress. When she wanted more, the affair ended. Until a pregnancy test changed everything...

Other titles from this new trilogy by Lucy Monroe
THE PRINCE'S VIRGIN WIFE—May
THE SCORSOLINI MARRIAGE BARGAIN—July

www.eHarlequin.com

HPRB0606